Perhaps It Was His Native American Blood That Told Him To Claim His Woman, To Keep Her Near.

Two mornings ago Gabriel had awakened with Miranda in his arms. Was that a dream, the soft fragrance of her haunting him? In her, he'd seen his eternity and his essence, in that flashing pinpoint before his desire came flooding into her keeping. He'd known that he was meant to hold her, to give her his child, to keep her safe until the winds took away their breath—together. She'd burned a path to his heart, and that soft scar hurt him more deeply than those of the flesh.

Flesh? She was more—a part of him now, inside him, moving in his blood, heating it, the fever for her— Wait! Gabriel hadn't been aware of the power of a woman's calling to him. He wasn't certain about his strength against it now....

Dear Reader,

Welcome to the world of Silhouette Desire, where you can indulge yourself every month with romances that can only be described as passionate, powerful and provocative!

Popular author Cait London offers you *Gabriel's Gift,* this April's MAN OF THE MONTH. We're sure you'll love this tale of lovers once separated who reunite eighteen years later and must overcome the past before they can begin their future together.

The riveting Desire miniseries TEXAS CATTLEMAN'S CLUB: LONE STAR JEWELS continues with *Her Ardent Sheikh* by Kristi Gold, in which a dashing sheikh must protect a free-spirited American woman from danger.

In *Wife with Amnesia* by Metsy Hingle, the estranged husband of an amnesiac woman seeks to win back her love…and to save her from a mysterious assailant. Watch for Metsy Hingle's debut MIRA title, *The Wager,* in August 2001. Barbara McCauley's hero "wins" a woman in a poker game in *Reese's Wild Wager,* another tantalizing addition to her SECRETS! miniseries. Enjoy a contemporary "beauty and the beast" story with Amy J. Fetzer's *Taming the Beast.* And Ryanne Corey brings you a runaway heiress who takes a walk on the wild side with the bodyguard who's fallen head over heels for her in *The Heiress & the Bodyguard.*

Be sure to treat yourself this month, and read all six of these exhilarating Desire novels!

Enjoy!

Joan Marlow Golan

Joan Marlow Golan
Senior Editor, Silhouette Desire

Please address questions and book requests to:
Silhouette Reader Service
U.S.: 3010 Walden Ave., P.O. Box 1325, Buffalo, NY 14269
Canadian: P.O. Box 609, Fort Erie, Ont. L2A 5X3

Cait London
GABRIEL'S GIFT

Published by Silhouette Books
America's Publisher of Contemporary Romance

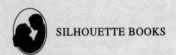 SILHOUETTE BOOKS

ISBN 0-373-76357-3

GABRIEL'S GIFT

Copyright © 2001 by Lois Kleinsasser

Visit Silhouette at www.eHarlequin.com

Printed in U.S.A.

Books by Cait London

CAIT LONDON

lives in the Missouri Ozarks but loves to travel the Northwest's gold rush/cattle drive trails every summer. She enjoys research trips, meeting people and going to Native American dances. Ms. London is an avid reader who loves to paint, play with computers and grow herbs (particularly scented geraniums right now). She's a national bestselling and award-winning author, and she has also written historical romances under another pseudonym. Three is her lucky number; she has three daughters, and the events in her life have always been in threes. "I love writing for Silhouette," Cait says. "One of the best perks about all this hard work is the thrilling reader response and the warm, snug sense that I have given readers an enjoyable, entertaining gift."

To Stella

Prologue

———

From the Journal of Magda Claas, Montana 1881

This beautiful valley, in the land the Indians call "Montana," and the women who have become my sisters, have given me peace and comfort. In the heat of that hot, dry summer, ten women came together in this beautiful valley with towering mountains on one side, a lake filled with fish, and lush green grass for our stock.

The land is wild and rough with men, who would take us as they would a cow or a horse, caring little for our pride. Who would protect us? we wondered by our campfire and wagons and stock, women without menfolk in a harsh land. We wanted husbands, of course, but we wanted the freedom to choose good men who would treat us well.

Fleur Arnaud, Anastasia Duscha, Beatrice Avril, Jasmine Dupree, China Belle Ruppurt, and Fancy Benjamin had already been treated poorly by their men. They would not settle for less than their rightful due again. Margaret Gertraud, Cynthia Whitehall and myself had not suffered so, but we were determined to keep ourselves free of unjoyful and painful bondage, such as they had suffered. We know little of the woman known as LaRue, except that she is most helpful and inventive. She has loved, she said, and she has lost. Yet her quiet, secret smile tells more.

So it was that women with strong minds decided to become a family, to protect one another, to weigh marriage offers as a father or brother would have done in the Old World, to see that men courted as was proper and that they kept their marriage promises. We decided that our family would protect the brides men would have, inspecting the men's qualifications as future husbands. At first, we laughed, and then the idea grew into our dream.

Jasmine Dupree had been berry picking when her baby decided to come, and an Indian man, Mr. Deerhorn, came to her rescue. He fashioned a *travois,* two long poles with a blanket between them, which dragged behind his horse, and brought her back to our camp. He was most shocked when Cynthia Whitehall of Boston society thanked him by kissing his cheek.

I am a midwife, and when Jasmine's baby

came into my hands, we cried. That night, we decided to name our valley Freedom, and our town, too. With the fine big boy nursing at Jasmine's breast, and joy in our hearts, we sat down to decide the Rules for Bride Courting. By next summer, we will have a town called Freedom.

Mr. Deerhorn came the next morning with a reed basket of herbs from his mother. He explained the uses to us, but his warm gaze followed Cynthia. A bold woman, she has become suddenly quiet.

Magda Claas, Midwife and Healer and
Butter Maker
Freedom Valley, Montana

One

My children are my joy. A widow with three young children, I feared I would fail them. Yet now Tanner, the oldest at twenty, is already off to college and has his heart set on Gwyneth Smith. At sixteen, Kylie is the youngest, and tosses herself into life. She is determined to bring down one Michael Cusack. My oldest daughter, Miranda, is just eighteen and furious with Gabriel Deerhorn. It has been months since he called or came to our house. Always controlled and keeping her secrets, Miranda will say nothing. I think she dreamed of marrying him, and now she is grimly determined to leave Freedom.

—from the journal of Anna Bennett,
descendant of Magda Claas

The woman stood in the night, campfire smoke curling around her and Gabriel's baby nestling in her rounded belly. Filled with promises and love, her hair swept back from her face by the mountain wind, her eyes were warm upon Gabriel. The joy that she gave him swirled through the tops of the pines, settled deeply within him. She had his heart and together they had made a child—

Gabriel awoke suddenly, his heart racing, his mind trying to hold the dream close to him. Yet it swirled off into the mountain's December snow, torn from him too soon. It was always the same, the woman who came to him in sleep, his child nestled within her. He sat up, his hands shaking as he stirred his campfire into life—not for the warmth, but to do something, anything. Gabriel lifted his face to the slashing mountain snow, then turned to study his evening campfire. The snowflakes blended with the smoke and disappeared, just as the woman always left him. Without her, he carried the cold ache of loneliness.

His people believed in dreams, in the meanings they held. Gabriel breathed deeply, and glanced at his horse in the pine bough shelter. The Appaloosa's mottled coat blended with the veil of snowflakes as the gelding returned Gabriel's study. Once the woman had come to Gabriel when he was cold and alone, curling warmly against him, placing his hand on her full breast. Milk for the coming child had dampened his palm and gave him peace; he knew that his blood would live on, his heritage and pride. He had dreamed of her riding in front of him, wrapped snugly in his arms. Turning slightly, she would lean against him, her breath warm upon his throat, their baby pressing against his stomach.

Gabriel shook his head and dusted the snowflakes from his face. Perhaps it was Michael Cusack and Kylie Bennett's approaching church wedding that had stirred the dreams, like dying embers brought back to life. Perhaps it was Tanner and Gwyneth's announcement of a coming baby. Gabriel hadn't thought of his need to have a child for years. At thirty-seven, he had settled into his mountain ranch, tending his horses and cattle and occasionally serving as a guide for tourists.

He shoved a stick into the fire, prodding it, and watched the coals spring into flame. He'd been too lonely at his cabin, and he'd known the woman would come to him where his Native American blood called to him and the dreams came more freely—in the high untamed mountains overlooking Freedom Valley.

He rose and walked to the rock bluff overlooking the valley with its twinkling lights. His ancestor had helped the women who founded their dream, a land and a town where they could choose their lives.

Just there was the Bennett farm, a tiny complete twenty acres. Mother of three children and a widow, Anna Bennett had lost her life almost a year ago, when her car collided with a semitruck. A midwife and healer, she was loved in Freedom Valley, respected by Gabriel's mother, also a midwife and healer. First Tanner Bennett had come home to claim his ex-wife, and then Kylie to clash with Michael Cusack. Miranda would be coming soon, Kylie's matron of honor.

Miranda. Gabriel breathed unsteadily, hunching down into his shearling coat, as her name curled in the wind. He was only nineteen to her seventeen when they started dating. In another year, Miranda had finished high school and colleges were courting her. Gabriel saw then that their lives were not meant to be entwined. For he was a part of this life, these high mountains, the livestock, the land and his blood.

For Miranda's good, he had torn her from him, never to hold that sweet scent of her close, those soft innocent lips against his.

He'd told her he didn't want her. The lie had hurt, because back then, he had wanted to go before the Women's Council and speak for her. He'd wanted to court her in the traditional way of his ancestors, to offer horses as a bridal price. But Miranda was meant for a different life, one apart from his. Intelligent, creative, and at the top of her class, Miranda would have resented him eventually.

When she'd visited Anna, Gabriel had seen her and the ache returned. She'd said she was happy, and that a few years ago she began living with a man she intended to marry. Gabriel lifted his face to the icy mountain wind. At thirty-five, Miranda was now probably married and a mother. He frowned slightly. Anna had been so proud of her children, and yet she had said nothing of Miranda's wedding or of grandchildren. A sensitive woman, perhaps Anna had known that information would trouble him.

He wasn't looking forward to seeing Miranda and her husband at Kylie's wedding. Gabriel stood suddenly and tore off his coat and the layers of clothing beneath it, giving himself to the freezing, cleansing winds. The wind tore at his hair, swirling it around his face in a storm of snowflakes, and he thought he heard the song of her low, soft voice.

He pushed her from his heart and still she clung to him—soft, warm, beckoning.

The first week of January, Miranda came down the wedding aisle before Kylie, the bride. Standing with the other men beside the groom—Michael Cusack— Gabriel held his breath. With a coronet of daisies in her sleek black hair, bound into a fashionable knot, Miranda caught his heart—just that easily, after all those years.

Taller than Kylie, Miranda moved with the same lithe grace, her flowing feminine gown of mauve emphasizing the blush on her cheeks. Those green eyes were just as startling, highlighted by the magic of makeup. Framed by those long sweeping lashes, her eyes still reminded him of the summer meadows in the mountains. Her brows, finely arched, were like that of the wings of the raven. The new softness in her face, much like Anna's, said she had found peace.

But her mouth— Gabriel tensed, pushing away the soft, haunting memory of it against his, the sweet hunger of seventeen-year-old Miranda.

Then she turned, taking the traditional matron-of-honor's place beside Kylie, and Gabriel's gaze locked on Miranda's gown, clinging to the slight mound of her belly.

There was no time like the present, Miranda thought, as she moved through the dancers, making her way to Gabriel. If she were going to make a home in Freedom Valley for her and her baby, she had to grapple with her "ghosts" first. Gabriel was definitely a man no woman could forget.

As a teenager, she'd had a crush on most of her brother's friends—some of them had married, but those who remained were called "the Bachelor Club" by the matrons of Freedom Valley. Those men who did not conform to the time-honored customs of the Founding Mothers of Freedom Valley were condemned as "Culls."

Gabriel was definitely not a "Cull." He was quiet, thoughtful and lived peacefully on his mountain ranch. He had never married and had been her first real love. At times, the sweetness of those memories caught her, wrapped carefully before she stored them again in the past. Standing with the other men at the altar, Gabriel had been just as tall and fierce and lean as she remembered. His dark suit emphasized that hawkish look, his hair in a rough, long cut and just touching his shoulders. His face was harder, more weathered and angular, tension humming from him. He wouldn't be comfortable in a suit, of course, but he had made the sacrifice for his friends.

She'd felt the burn of those black hunter's eyes, the narrowing of them on her rounded belly. Had his hard mouth tightened then, or had she just imagined that reaction? Gabriel always held his emotions tightly, even at nineteen, when his body ran warm and taut with the need to take more….

Miranda fought the tremble moving through her, and stopped her hand from nervously fidgeting with her hair. She wouldn't be nervous of Gabriel Deerhorn, no matter how fiercely he'd scowled at her.

Again—had she just imagined his reaction? Or was it a reflection of her own shaken emotions?

Standing in front of him now, Miranda looked up. His black eyes were flat, shielded now, deep set beneath those fierce brows. The lights gleamed on his high cheekbones, the planes and shadows of his face cruising along an unrelenting jaw and a chin with a magical little dimple. For just a heartbeat, the memory of his unsteady breath sweeping across her cheek, the open hot furnace of that mouth, startled her.

There had been no softness in that long, well-shaped mouth the day he told her that he didn't want her.

Miranda pushed away that slicing memory and decided to keep their meeting light. "I've danced with all the other men in the Bachelor Club. You're next and it's the last dance."

Gabriel looked over her head, ignoring her. Then those black eyes pounced upon her, tearing at her, though his deep voice still held that magical lilt. She didn't understand that slashing glance, battering her, and it was quickly shielded into a bland expression. "Sure."

He took her stiffly in his arms, in the traditional way she remembered, and eased her into the waltz. She'd forgotten that he was so tall—six foot three— and with the added height of his polished Western boots, she barely reached his shoulder. He had that ramrod-straight look of a lean working man, and for just a moment, she imagined him on horseback, his body flowing easily with the animal's.

As a teenager, he'd been so careful of her sensibilities. The first time she saw him playing field football without his shirt, she'd been entranced by the beauty of his smooth, dark skin rippling over the muscles and cords.

Now his hand was rough against hers, his shoulders even wider, and she felt feminine and delicate within his very proper embrace. She wondered what had happened to that sense of being a woman—had it been stripped away by her career, in the push-push to succeed? She dressed and acted like a woman, but inside she felt so empty—except for the wonder of her coming baby. Miranda glanced up at Gabriel, dancing as if forced to do his duty. He'd given her the only wildflower bouquet she'd ever had, but now those high, sharp cheekbones and that jaw looked as if none of the boy's softness remained. She wondered what bitterness had happened to him, to make those lines upon his brow, the brackets beside his lips. Strength ran through his body, though he held her lightly. She could sense the vibrations of emotions circling him, that taut hoarding of his thoughts, the control she always associated with him. "Michael and Kylie are so perfect for each other, don't you think?" she asked, just to hear him speak.

"Sure." A man obligated to dance with his friend's sister, Gabriel looked over her head, studying the other dancers.

Gabriel was simply doing his duty, dancing with her, and Miranda gave in to the impish need to prick that cool shield. "I hear you have a ranch now, and that you guide like your father did."

"Sure. He's retired now." He looked down at her, and his hard face softened momentarily. "I'm sorry about your mother. I liked Anna."

Suddenly he seemed so safe, even after all the years between. She couldn't resist placing her forehead against his shoulder and resting there for just a moment, her hand clenching his large callused one as an anchor. Gabriel tensed, his hand at her back opening, digging in slightly. Was he afraid she'd cry? That a pregnant woman's moods would embarrass him? Unpredictable emotions seemed to be the effect of her pregnancy, so unlike Miranda's usual control. She was too vulnerable now because she'd fought reality and lost. The man she'd thought she would marry didn't want her or their baby.

Only Kylie and Tanner, her brother, knew that she wasn't married, that her child was unwanted by its father. She'd come to Freedom to protect her baby, to surround it with love and family. She'd stay in her mother's home, find work and nurture her child. Freedom Valley was where she belonged; somehow she'd find a way to explain the missing husband, and in two months she'd be holding her baby. She'd only been back two days, but amid the hustle of the traditional wedding Michael Cusack wanted for Kylie, Miranda knew she had made the right choice—to come back home. She'd sold everything of her past life, wanting a new one for herself and her baby.

After living together for three years and finally planning a wedding, Scott wasn't prepared for the changes in her body, her brief morning sickness had repelled him. He'd wanted a family earlier, but then suddenly—with the wedding a month away—he explained how trapped he felt by her and the impending marriage, and the child he didn't want. He blamed her nesting urges for ruining a "good setup."

"Do you want to rest?" Gabriel asked softly above her head. That liquid deep voice was the same, calming, gentling...

Unwilling to leave the safety of his shoulder, Miranda shook her head. "I'm sorry. I wish Mom could have been here."

Her mother's fatal accident had stirred her need to marry, to have children, to carry on with life. She couldn't blame Scott. He was clearly surprised by his own fears. They'd had a good relationship, blending their work and lives. It wasn't a blinding love affair, but she had settled for a workable and pleasant one with Scott. Yet, there it was—a solid lump of the ugly unexpected. Scott did not want to be a father; he couldn't bear to look at her, or touch her, after the six-weeks' pregnancy test proved positive. He'd been almost physically ill at the news.

The plain gold band on her finger was a lie, and looking back, so was her life with Scott. She'd desperately needed her mother's home in which to mend, to be strong for her baby. With Tanner and Kylie living nearby, Miranda's baby would always have a family and safety.

The music ended and still Gabriel held her, unmoving. She caught the scent of wood smoke and horses and leather and man, all safe and good. Slowly she lifted her head to meet those searching black eyes. "I'm fine," she managed to say and forced herself to ease away from the first safety she'd felt in months. "Thank you."

"Sure." Gabriel stood very still, watching her, and Miranda couldn't bear to meet his gaze.

Then Sadie McGinnis, a member of the Women's

Council, came to her side. "Your husband couldn't
get away for the wedding, hmm?"

Miranda shook her head no, and hated the lie. "Excuse me. It's time to catch Kylie's bouquet."

"But, honey. That's for the unmarried girls," Sadie
said firmly.

"Oh, yes. Of course. But I want to see better."
Miranda moved away quickly. Did anyone suspect?
Amid the cheers, she glanced at the people she'd
known all of her life. She found only joy and warmth
in their expressions. Gabriel stood apart, his face unreadable, and she wondered if he knew that she was
alone.

Somehow, she'd get through her unsteady emotions, Miranda thought in the silence of her mother's
home. In Seattle, she'd used her analytical mind to
dissect statistics, to determine potential markets. A
high-paid executive with a magna cum laude degree,
she'd plunged through daily routines, gauging her life
by clocks and corporate demands. Scott had been a
comfortable part of that life, those routines.

Who was she? Where was that cool reasoning
power now? she wondered, as she foundered in her
emotions. She sat by the opened hope chest she'd
filled all those years ago. She'd dreamed of being
Gabriel's wife, of having his children. Hope chests
were a requirement of the brides in Freedom Valley,
and her mother had helped her fill this one. Miranda
smoothed the tiny hand-stitched quilt her mother had
made, the note pinned to it. "With love, Grandma."

Miranda scrubbed the tears from her face, then

gave way to crying. "I need you, Mom. Why did that accident have to happen?"

The house she'd grown up in was too quiet, the shadows echoing with Tanner's outraged shouts as he tore after two younger sisters. Kylie's giggles curled through the years, and their mother's soothing voice: "You'll be fine. Just do what's right and everything else will follow."

Miranda smoothed the baby blanket Juanita Deerhorn, Gabriel's mother, had stitched long ago. When Gabriel and Miranda were teenagers, Juanita simply came to Anna's house one morning with a wrapped present for Miranda. One of Juanita's famous saucer-size red roses had been tucked into the ribbon binding the gift. A Southern woman of grace and charm, Juanita's birth name had been Lillian. But the elder Deerhorns affectionately referred to her in a name more familiar to them—"Juanita."

Juanita had been unusually serious that morning. "My mother-in-law, Gabriel's grandmother, White Fawn, told me to make this for you. I always do what she tells me, for she usually has a reason. I hope you like it."

The baby blanket was for Miranda's hope chest, dainty hand stitching fashioning a Celtic-looking design of interwoven circles with no beginning and no end. Juanita's smile had been soft as she traced them. "The batting was from White Fawn's sheep. She hand-carded it and drew the design for me to use. Don't make too much of this, honey. White Fawn often tells me these small things to do, and because you are such a lovely girl, and I love your dear mother, this is a gift of the heart, not because I exactly expect you to be toting my grandchild someday.''

The blanket had remained in Miranda's hope chest, the rose carefully pressed with it.... She pressed her hand against the small kick in her womb. The baby seemed weaker in the past few days, but perhaps that was the stress of leaving her old life. Easing downstairs, Miranda suddenly felt very old and worn, as though she'd crossed centuries, not a hectic month of making arrangements to move to Freedom Valley.

She brewed a cup of tea and settled comfortably under the afghan on her mother's couch. Her mother was still here, in the scents and herbs, though Gwyneth and Kylie and Tanner had tended and cleaned the house. In the spring, the yellow tulips and irises and lavender beds would sprout, the tender herbs scenting the air.

Tanner and Kylie had each returned to Freedom Valley, and each had lived in Anna's home. Its warmth circled Miranda now, giving her the shelter she needed. But one day, the contents would have to be separated, each sister and Tanner taking a bit home with them.

"My doctor said the baby is perfectly healthy," Miranda quietly reassured herself amid the still shadows of the house. *"But oh, Mom. I wish you were here."* Miranda decided to rest before checking in with Freedom Valley's doctor and tried not to cry, a brief release for all the emotions storming her. She was simply too tired to drag herself into the reality of her new life in Freedom Valley just yet.

Tanner and Gwyneth's baby would arrive after hers, and the cousins would be family. Kylie and Michael wouldn't wait to start a family, because Kylie never waited, forever leaping into life. Her brother and sister were blissfully happy in their new lives and their mother would have loved keeping her grandchildren.

Her mother's death had pricked Miranda's biological need for a child, a new life to replace a dear one that had been cut short. The continuity of Anna's life was important, and so, safe in the knowledge that Scott would want their child, Miranda had conceived. Looking back, while she was grieving over her mother was not the best time to make a decision to have a baby. Miranda smoothed her belly and knew that she had enough love for two parents.

"Mother? Where are you?" Miranda whispered, and ached when no answer returned from the shadows. She looked outside to the snow slashing across her mother's front porch. Anna had always fed the birds early in the morning, and filling the many bird feeders would be a start for Miranda's routine. Day by day, she'd build a life for her child that was safe and good. Just now, she wasn't ready to expose herself to anyone but Kylie and Tanner. But eventually she would have to deal with gossip. A younger, more vulnerable Miranda had already handled rumors and sympathetic looks by Freedom Valley's townfolk.

All those years ago, teenage Gabriel had hurt her terribly. "I don't want you. Don't even think of marriage between us, or anything else," he'd said grimly. She'd cried horribly, hiding from her family, trying not to show her pain. *He'd torn away her heart and deep inside she'd hated him, vowing never to forgive him.*

Years later, another man's confession had jolted
her. She'd been startled by Scott's reaction and rejec-
tion, but not hurt. It was as if her emotions with him
hadn't been deep enough to wound. He'd been truthful, though, and she admired that more than a man
who forced himself to submit to a life he didn't want.

Miranda slid down on the couch, snuggling into the
familiar warmth of her homecoming. She closed her
eyes and wondered why she could not remember the
Nordic texture of Scott's crisp waving blond hair, and
yet the coarse, straight texture of Gabriel's black
shaggy mane seemed so familiar.

Was he happy? Gossip said he hadn't married, that
he kept to himself and his mountains. Miranda
frowned and closed her eyes wearily, her hand
smoothing the baby nestled within her. Why did he
seem so uncomfortable with her? Did those sweet
days of their teenage years still curl around him as
they did her? *Gabriel, you look so hard and lonely.
What happened to you?* Then, a tiny kick beneath her
hand claimed her thoughts of the future.

Two

The most gentle of hearts can be found in unsuspecting places. Women tend to think that only another woman can give comfort, but men—given the chance—can offer kindness to a troubled heart.

Anna Bennett's Journal

Gabriel followed the snowplow as it passed Anna's small farm, leaving small mountains of snow on either side of the road. Departing immediately after their wedding for their honeymoon, Kylie and Michael had missed the heavy snow that now bent the trees and blocked some roads and airports. The light lacy snowflakes hit Gabriel's windshield and the *clack-clack* of his wipers created the pattern for his thoughts.

After the wedding, he had packed a two-week sup-

ply of groceries into his battered Jeep. Then he had
settled down with his friends at the Silver Dollar Tavern, the site of the wedding reception. He was more
comfortable there, with the loud country music and
the smells, than in the church, with a tie tight around
his neck. The sounds had vibrated in the tavern's
smoky room, a jarring contrast to his very quiet, solitary log home. Though he visited Tanner and his life-
long friends throughout the year, Gabriel was always
glad to get back to his mountains. The Bachelor
Club—Koby, Fletcher, Dylan, Brody and the rest of
his friends—had toasted their ''dying breed.'' Because Dakota Jones's little sister, Karolina, alias ''Su-
per Snoop,'' had been in a snit, mourning her ''old
maid'' status, the men had taken turns dancing with
her. But Gabriel had danced the last dance with Miranda. Another time, when a woman would ask a man
for the last dance, it would mean she chose him for
her future husband. Gabriel wasn't likely to follow
the local customs—love had passed him by, and he'd
settled for peace in the mountains.

Later, only a little of the tension remained from
holding Miranda in his arms. He'd stayed the night
at Michael's house, the newlyweds bound for a sunny,
tropical honeymoon.

Filled with thoughts of yesterday's wedding and
seeing Miranda again, he kept his four-wheel-drive
Jeep a respectable distance behind the snowplow. At
six o'clock in the morning, the flashing red light of
the snowplow shot off into the darkness. Behind the
wheel of the charging beast, Mac Reno would be in
an evil mood, pained by a Saturday night hangover.
Mac had once gotten in an argument with Willa, the

owner of the Wagon Wheel Café and the mayor of
Freedom; he'd used the snowplow to bury her car.

After the joy of Kylie and Michael yesterday, and
Gwyneth and Tanner's delight in their coming baby,
Gabriel's solitary life seemed as gray as the morning.
The woman in the smoke—her eyes warm upon him,
and her body rounded with his child—was only a
dream he used to fill the ache inside him, a self-
induced medicine to give him momentary peace. He'd
made the right decision when they were teenagers—

Gabriel ran his hand over his jaw, the sound of the
scrape as raw as his emotions. He didn't like being
unsettled, tossed back into the past when Miranda
danced close and sweet against him. She wore another
man's ring, and now she carried his child— Why had
that shadow crossed her face when asked about her
husband?

Gabriel's hands tightened on the steering wheel. If
she had been mistreated— He pushed away that ugly
thought. She looked as if she were blooming, the
pregnancy sitting well on her.

But she had leaned against him in the old way,
when troubles came too deeply upon her. As a boy,
he'd been stunned that she would give so much to
him, letting him see her doubts and trusting him with
her thoughts. She'd grieved then for her father, Paul,
a good man who had died of a terminal disease.

*Miranda smelled the same—of sun and wind brush-
ing across the lush sweet-grass meadows. Her eyes
were still the shining green of new grass, clear and
bright and happy—she'd looked that way when he'd
given her that wildflower bouquet all those years ago.
Now she was a woman, preparing for her child, and*

yet she seemed so fragile, light and willowy in his arms. He feared holding her too close, keeping his distance, for just then, he was uncertain of himself.

Gabriel glanced at Anna's driveway, at the snow the plow had piled high, barring the entrance. Out of habit, he eased the Jeep over the snow and reached to the back to push aside the snowshoes resting over his shovel. Anna had always been good to him, and he was only one of many who would clear her driveway. In no hurry to return to his empty house, Gabriel glanced at Anna's home and found light streaming from all the windows, creating golden patches into the gray dawn. The house was much like Anna had left it a year ago, though both Tanner and Kylie had taken turns living in it. Tanner had explained that none of Anna's children could bear separating her things. Filled with warm scents and Anna's tender presence, the house would be a ghost to Miranda now. She would be doing her prowling, missing her mother, and that wound would be slow to heal. How could her husband not see to her at such a time, not come with her? To know such a woman and not care for her was unthinkable.

But then Miranda was her own woman, very independent, and it wasn't for Gabriel to mull her life.

When he opened the Jeep's door, the freezing temperatures hit him. He sucked in the icy air, letting it cleanse him, and then began to shovel the snow. The earth needed snow for nourishment, and to make the grass grow lush and green— Miranda's eyes were still as green, softer now with her coming baby nestled inside her. The thought jarred him, how easily she stepped into his mind after all those years. Perhaps she had always been there.

The image of her teenage disbelief slashed across him. In curt terms, he'd told her that they weren't meant for each other and that she should take the scholarship offers coming to her, that she should leave Freedom Valley. He'd told her that their paths were not meant to be one—that his life's path was not for her—and the shock in those green eyes had shamed him. Her slender body had recoiled as if taking a physical blow. Though his heart had been tearing, he tried not to show his anguish and how much her tears hurt him. The memory added force to his shovel's blow against a shrub, shaking the branches and dislodging the heavy snow before it could break them. He tempered the other blows, pushing the shattering image into the past for a time.

The birds began to chirp and he smiled briefly. Anna's feeders were always kept well filled and suet balls hung from the trees. Coming from a close family, Miranda would honor her mother's desires. When would she leave? Would he see her again?

Gabriel thrust the unseemly thoughts from him. She was another man's woman, and it was not his way to— In the stillness of morning, a soft moan sounded amid the chirping birds, and there at the base of Anna's front steps was—

Gabriel ran toward Miranda, curled into a ball. Birdseed was scattered on the snow, and the skid mark on the icy top step told the story. Tearing off his leather gloves, he crouched to her side. He eased away the corner of her shawl and found her face too white, a thin trickle of blood at her forehead.

How long had she lain in the freezing temperatures? Trembling, Gabriel eased his arm beneath her head. "Miranda?"

His heart stopped beating while he waited for her to answer. "Miranda?"

This time she moaned slightly and tensed, as if in pain. When she moved, Gabriel saw the blood soaking the white snow. He eased away her long, heavy coat and grimly acknowledged the likelihood that Miranda had lost her baby. "Shh, Miranda," he whispered as he began to work quickly.

Through the pain tearing at her body, Miranda looked up at Gabriel's darkly weathered face. He looked so tired and worried, his black eyes soft and warm upon her. "Miranda?"

Her head throbbed, and the cold cloth on her forehead came away with her blood. She remembered falling, trying to protect her baby and icy terror leaped into her. *"My baby?"*

"Miranda, you're in Anna's house. Upstairs in your bedroom—"

She reached to snag his flannel shirt, to fist it with both hands. "Tell me."

"Miranda, you have to help me. The roads are closed and the doctor can't get here soon. You have to tell me what to do. Mother is a midwife, but I can't reach her. You helped your mother at times like this. You've got to think—"

"My baby?" she cried again and knew from the emptiness inside her that the baby had come too soon.

Gabriel took her hands in his and shook his head. "I tried. He was a fine boy."

Her wail ripped through the still shadows. Or was that the sound of her heart and soul tearing apart? *Oh my little love, wait for me…Mommy will take care of you…wait for me…*

"Miranda, come back to me," Gabriel said firmly. "Tell me what to do. The doctor told me some of it, but you know what your mother would have done. Where are Tanner and Gwyneth? They're not answering their telephone."

She shook her head, fighting against reality and pain. Tears burned her eyes and she remembered how cold she'd been, how the baby— *The fall was her fault.* Her baby would have lived except for her need to start a daily routine, to feed the birds. Her voice was rusty, thin and seemed to come from someone else. "They decided to spend the night in a resort hotel."

It wasn't true. Her baby was still… The pain slapped at her, no worse than her grief, her heart and body crying for that little, precious life.

"Tell me what to do," Gabriel repeated softly, firmly. "You need attention."

Tiredly, without emotion, her voice coming from far away, she instructed Gabriel how to help her. He drew off her soiled clothing, replacing her pajamas with a warm soft flannel shirt and nothing else. In her grief, she felt no shame. Gabriel spoke to her softly, soothingly, his manner impersonal as he changed her toweling and lifted her hips. His callused hand laid on her forehead, anchoring her as she grieved. "I will bring your son to you. Do you want to see him?"

"Yes," she whispered, the emptiness of her womb aching. She wanted just one moment before the doc-

tor arrived and officially declared the medical reality.
How could this tiny, perfect life be torn from her?
Oh, my little baby—

Gabriel had cleansed her baby, holding the tiny
body close against him. "His father will want to
know. Do you want me to call him?"

"No! My baby is mine alone." She couldn't bear
to share anything of her baby with the man who didn't
want him. She met Gabriel's frown and the truth tore
from her. "I'm not married. Scott couldn't bear the
thought of marriage or children. The changes in my
body repulsed him. He tried not to show it, but he
couldn't bear to touch me. I couldn't bear the thought
of a baby raised by a father who resented being
trapped. I came home to Freedom Valley to keep my
baby safe—"

She tugged the wedding band she'd purchased from
her finger, hurling it against the wall. It bounced and
fell, rolling across the floor as empty as her life now.

She tensed as Gabriel sat, holding the tiny baby
close and safe against him. "He's a fine son. A man
would be honored to know that you carried his
child."

Miranda turned her face away from the tender
sight. Gabriel was a man meant to hold and love children; he wouldn't understand Scott's fear.

"A fine son... For a man's blood to continue gives
him greatness. To have a woman give him such a
child is a treasure most men would honor. I have
longed for a son, or a daughter," he added as a gentle
afterthought. "My arms need a child in them. I know
this in my heart, but yet I cannot—"

She turned suddenly to him, rage and pain searing

her. She didn't hide her torment from Gabriel, a man she'd known all her life. Tossed by her emotions, she was angry with him, for tearing them apart. Gabriel would have been a perfect father and yet he hadn't wanted her, either. "Did you hear me? Scott did *not* want me, or my baby."

"Who do you grieve for—yourself, or your child?" The quiet, thoughtful challenge took her back and she turned away again. "A woman carrying a child is beautiful. I thought at the wedding how you glowed, how you seemed to have the sunlight inside you."

Gabriel pushed away the rage within him. How could any man not be at the side of the woman carrying his child? Yet he forced himself to calm, for Miranda was too pale and vulnerable now. Her eyes were shadowed, dark circles beneath them. Her mouth quivered, those beautiful eyes brimming with tears and the pulse in her throat beating heavily with emotion. She held her child for a while, and then he eased it away.

She looked outside at the snowstorm, too silent, her grief etched in her pale features, the tears dripping from her cheeks. "I don't blame Scott. He was as surprised at his reaction as I was."

Gabriel damned the weakness of her lover. Holding him blameless, she must still love him. Perhaps she wanted him still, wishing for him to come claim her. Gabriel pushed away that slight, unexpected burn of jealousy; Miranda needed his strength now. "Your mother would want you here, Miranda. Can you feel her?"

"Yes," she said tiredly. "I can. I hurt, Gabriel. Every part of me and I feel so empty and so cold."

"You're badly bruised, Miranda. You must have fallen from the top step, and you were lying in the snow for a time. The cold probably slowed the loss of blood." Gabriel inhaled sharply. He placed his hand over her forehead, testing its warmth, and then he took her pulse. "I'm going to call the doctor to see what else I can do. Then would you like me to lie with you, to hold you?"

In her pain, she'd lost all sense of modesty and she was feeling too weak, too vulnerable now. Where was the strong controlled woman she'd always been, always—? Now she only felt the need for life. "Just for a little bit. I need to feel—a heartbeat other than mine."

Miranda gave herself to the warmth of Gabriel's gentle hands and voice and when he settled beside her, she slid off into a welcoming darkness. Then someone was shaking her lightly, and Gabriel was bending over her, cupping her face with his big, callused hands. His voice was low and urgent. "Miranda, listen to me. The doctor is almost here. Will you trust me? I am only thinking of you now and your baby and of your mother. I want to smooth this road for you."

She shook her head, unwilling to agree to anything but the truth. Then Gabriel took her hand, wrapping it in his warm, strong one. "It is in my heart to protect you and your baby. Do you trust me?"

His eyes were kind and concerned and she had nowhere else to go, nothing— She gripped his hand, nodded slowly and slid back into sleep.

* * *

Gabriel. Through a window in her mother's house, Miranda watched the birds feed outside, gay in the dazzling midmorning light. Gabriel had been in the ambulance with her, staying in the small room at Freedom's clinic with her. "She carried my baby," she'd heard him say. "A fine son.... We had an argument and were working on our problems...."

The elderly nurse, Sarah, had been a friend of Anna's and hadn't spared Gabriel in her searing denouncement of "irresponsible males." He'd nodded solemnly, taking the tongue-lashing without comment. "I see she's not wearing her ring. She probably only purchased it to prevent gossip about her baby. Women have a sense of honor, even if *some* men do not," Sarah had stated pointedly.

Gabriel's plan was so old-fashioned, Miranda mused, giving his protection to her. Yet just then, she'd needed someone to lean on, the months of struggling with her failure—her misplaced trust in a man frightened so badly by marriage and children— and it was only too easy to let Gabriel handle everything. While the Bennetts were well respected in Freedom, Miranda didn't feel like explaining her past life, or the reason she was in Freedom now, without a husband. With Gabriel, Tanner and Kylie's solid fronts, she was well insulated against those who would gossip.

As the birds outside flitted around the feeders, swooping to the snow to pick at the fallen seeds, she pushed away the teardrop on her cheek. She was weak and uncomfortable and grieving and she didn't like herself now.

How could she have been so wrong about Scott? He'd been the perfect companion, a friend.

Why hadn't she been more careful that morning?

Miranda traced the window, mid-January's temperatures icy upon her fingertip. How strange that Tanner and Kylie would agree that Gabriel's plan was good for her. She shook her head. She was usually so strong and in control and now she seemed without an anchor. Miranda ran her cold fingertip across the tiny fresh scar on her forehead. The doctor's words of two weeks ago kept running through her mind. "A slight concussion… A premature delivery…"

She scrubbed her hands across her face and knew that she had to do something, anything to reclaim herself. Miranda suddenly closed her eyes. *How could she reclaim herself when every time she saw Gwyneth's softly rounded body, she thought of…?*

Her mother's house seemed so empty now, her crocheting basket just as she left it. A smoothly worn hook was still poised in the loop of white thread and anchored into the large spool. The image seemed symbolic, for Miranda was held in a moment of her life, unable to move on. She placed her hand over the spool of crochet thread, the hook and the half-finished doily. Her hand drifted across her body and she forced it to lift away from the emptiness. She had to go on, to make a life, and stop worrying Tanner and Kylie. Miranda inhaled the scent of her mother's lemon and beeswax furniture oil, and knew it was time to get to work. Her mother's pantry was a perfect place to start.

Kylie and Gwyneth could not empty Anna's canning jars, the green beans lined carefully on the shelf. After the thin years of widowhood and bringing up three children alone, Anna wouldn't have liked the waste. But she'd kept a tight eye on dated foodstuffs and the labels proved that the filled jars were past due. Tying on Anna's big work apron over her sweater and jeans, Miranda set out to clean her mother's pantry.

Tanner and Kylie and she had agreed months after Anna's accident that they would return to separate her things. Yet everything, except for the absence of Kylie's hope chest, was the same. Miranda inhaled slowly; the house couldn't remain as it was forever. Nothing was forever.... Kylie and Tanner were deep in their own lives, in the families that would come. She had to have a purpose—she'd always had goals, living her life by fulfilling them—and now she had nothing but her mother's pantry.

Gabriel shoveled the new snow in the driveway and then worked his way up Anna's walkway. He carefully cleaned the front steps and then circled the house, noting the light in the kitchen. After Miranda's family returned, he had eased away, letting them comfort her. But her eyes filled with pain at the sight of Gwyneth's rounded belly, and he knew that the healing would be long and painful. From others, he knew that Miranda hadn't left her mother's house.

Perhaps she mourned the man who couldn't bear the shackles of marriage or children. Perhaps she waited for him to come to her. It wasn't Gabriel's place to stay with her, but he came down from the mountains every two days, trekking the first bit with his snowshoes to shovel snow and tidy the limbs broken by the snow's weight. Miranda's car, a compact hatchback wagon, hadn't left Anna's driveway. The only marks were those by the Boat Shop, the building near Anna's house where Tanner fashioned custom-made wooden boats. Emotionally stripped, Miranda hadn't changed from the silent shadow of herself, and Gabriel wondered how she would react to his offer.

Was it for her welfare, or his own? Was he being selfish? Wanting to care for her, to be with her a little longer, before she left again?

To be truthful, Gabriel admitted to himself, the offer he would propose to Miranda suited his own needs to be close to her, to cherish her.

She didn't want to answer the quiet firm knock at the back porch door. One look through the window and she recognized Gabriel's height and broad shoulders. He'd come to shovel snow before, leaving as silently as he came. Wearily she opened the door to him. He'd seen everything, knew the ugly truth about a man who couldn't bear to look at her. But courtesy in her mother's house had always been observed. Those watchful black eyes traced the circles beneath her eyes, her pale coloring, and the large dampened apron. He knew too much for her to deny her mental state; she felt as if he could see into her mind, the storms battering and draining her. "So I'm depressed. It happens. I'll deal with it. Come in."

Gabriel stamped the snow from his boots and stepped into the back porch. Careful of Anna's floors, he sat on an old chair and unlaced his boots, removing them. In the kitchen, he eased off his coat and draped it methodically, thoughtfully, over the back of a chair. He took in the empty jars on the table, the contents dumped into a five-gallon bucket, the jars in the soapy water and ranging across the counters. Without speaking, he lifted the bucket and carried it to the back. He replaced his boots and carried the bucket outside. Miranda returned to washing jars, meticulously scrubbing them, holding them up to the kitchen window and inspecting them. If she could, she'd wash away the past as easily.

Gabriel returned with the empty bucket and stood watching her. Empty, she thought, comparing the bucket to how she felt. She avoided his gaze; he'd already seen too much of her life. Struggling against crying, Miranda turned to him. "It's an ordinary thing to do, isn't it? Cleaning jars? I have to do something…Gabriel, there was no need for you to feel you had to protect me."

She was angry now, with herself, with Scott, with Gabriel, with life. Her emotions swung from grief, to frustration, to self-pity, and back to anger. "I've always managed. I want to return something to you. Your mother made it for me years ago."

Hurrying upstairs, Miranda tore into her old hope chest, retrieving the baby blanket Juanita had made. She returned and handed it to Gabriel. She wanted him and everything about him stripped from her. "You should have this."

"Is it so hard to give yourself into the care of another?" he asked quietly, smoothing his large, strong fingers across the delicate stitching.

"She isn't here, Gabriel. *My mother was always here, and now she isn't.*" Illogical and grieving and emotional, Miranda served him the truth.

"She has done her work. Let her rest." Gabriel's

voice was deep and soothing, that slight lilt unique and magical. "Have you eaten?"

"Does it matter?" She was bitter and alone and detested herself now, for lashing out at a man who had helped her.

"Come with me to the café, Miranda. Eat with me. Let people see you are a woman of pride and strength, for Anna."

"That would only reinforce your lie, that you were the father of my baby, trying to reclaim me."

"You can tell them it is a lie, if you wish. I wanted to protect you then. I still do." He smiled softly, his hand smoothing her rumpled hair. She moved away, wary of Gabriel, who overpowered her mother's sunlit kitchen. "Because if you will allow me, I would like to ask for you at the Women's Council."

Miranda closed her eyes, his offer echoing in her head. She gripped the kitchen counter for an anchor. "I didn't hear that."

He placed his hand on her head and shook it lightly. The gesture was familiar, one her brother and his friends had used for a younger sister. "Open your eyes, little Miranda. It is a logical plan."

Little Miranda. He'd called her that so long ago....

She stared up at him, trying to mentally jump from a man who'd run from responsibility to the man wanting it. What did Gabriel stand to gain? Why would he want to protect her so dramatically, creating a lie that damaged his honor in Freedom Valley? "Tanner put you up to this. He was always—"

"He's worried. You are only human, Miranda, and dealing with too much all at once. You need a place apart from here to heal. I am offering my home. It is quiet and you would have time to adjust.''

Adjust? How? She shook her head. ''No.''

His body stiffened. ''Because you do not trust me?''

She met his eyes, fierce and black now with pride, the scowl darkening his hard face, the gleaming skin taut across those sharp, high cheekbones. ''I have always trusted you, even when you were such a rat and broke up with me. I could visit you, Gabriel. I would like that. But the Women's Council is for marriage offers and I see no reason to deceive anyone any longer.''

''I do. Let me share your burden. Let me give you shelter in all ways while you heal. For the most part, Freedom Valley has kind hearts, but there are tongues who would slice and hurt. Anna would not like that.''

Miranda's head began to throb, part of her wanting to leap into Gabriel's offer to let someone else deal with her own affairs. But reality said that she was a woman who could and should manage her life. ''The idea is tempting, but I couldn't let you offer for marriage. I have to handle this on my own.''

''But my pride will not let me do less. It is only a temporary means to help us both. The custom allows you my protection and my honor would not allow me to do less. I will only live with a woman under the custom of Freedom Valley—the trial marriage gives me a bit of company until spring, and hopefully, you'll relax and think and heal.''

Gabriel ruffled her hair slightly, his fingers drawing away a strand before leaving her. A smile lurked around his eyes and lips. ''With you in my home, my sister Clarissa would stop nagging me to get married. You'd be my protection.''

"You're offering me a distraction, Gabriel. I'll have to face life sometime." Yet his idea warmed her, a temporary reprieve.

"True. While you're thinking about it, let's go down to the Wagon Wheel and eat."

Three

Even the most levelheaded woman will be shaken by a man's honorable and sweet intentions to claim her. I long for the day my Miranda sees such a man coming for her in the old traditional ways of my mother and her mother before her. She guards her heart well, now that Gabriel is not in her wedding sights. His ancestor would not court Cynthia Whitehall of the Founding Mothers all those years ago. Though they married others, Cynthia was said never to glow again as she had when she looked at Mr. Deerhorn. I want my Miranda to glow and to dream as is any woman's right. It seems that now she has sealed her heart away. I wonder what can bring her back to life and love.

Anna Bennett's Journal

"**I**'d like to handle my own problems," Miranda whispered fiercely as she sat across from Gabriel at the Wagon Wheel Café. Her edges were showing now to a man who already knew too much about her. The falsely admitted father of her baby, Gabriel had stoically taken an amount of verbal battering from the traditional community. Though he seemed undisturbed, Miranda felt guilty, another emotion she couldn't afford. She hated her weakness now, feeling as though one more blow would shatter her like glass. "I know I'm not myself now, but I will be. I don't need your sympathy. You're asking me to live with you and let everyone think that we're trying to work out a nonexistent relationship. This is today, Gabriel, not a century and a half ago. Women have children— and lose them, and tend their own lives. I will…I will when I'm good and ready."

Gabriel nodded and leaned back in the booth, a tall broad-shouldered man, one long leg stretched outside the enclosure. The rich tone of his weathered skin reflected his Native American ancestry. The rough cut of his hair rested on the collar of his dark red sweater, those jarring fierce features locked into an unreadable mask. He'd dressed carefully, his jeans new and pressed into a sharp crease. His big hands framed the café's coffee cup, making the thick porcelain appear delicate. "I am not offering you a fancy resort in which to rest, Miranda. I built my home with few luxuries. You eat little. You can't grow strong without good food. You should eat what Gwyneth and Kylie bring you."

"I'm not hungry." Her stomach ached now, unused to the warm, nourishing "blue plate special" of roast beef, mashed potatoes and green beans. In front of her, a wedge of Willa's famed apple pie stood untouched.

"Are you going to eat that?" he asked and when she shook her head Gabriel ate her serving. "I like to eat with someone," he said quietly. "Do you?"

She shrugged and glanced at Willa, the owner of the café, who was eyeing Luigi of the Pasta Palace down the street. Luigi had once burst into an emotional Italian song that clearly marked his intentions to court Willa, a seasoned widow of many years. Luigi's huge drooping moustache was twitching as he smiled at Willa, his teeth gleaming whitely.

Following Miranda's look, Gabriel noted, "He's got her on the run."

"That's what people will say about you and me, Gabriel." Miranda's tone was hushed and fierce. She didn't want his kindness; she wanted to retreat. "This is all a sham. They'll think you *want* me. I don't feel right about this—my mother believed in the traditional courting customs here. I shouldn't have agreed to the lie about my life. I've managed so far without your protection."

Bitter? Ungrateful? She was all of that and guilty, too. Gabriel didn't deserve her harsh tirade. "I'm not exactly a likable person now. I'm sorry."

"Anna understood a great many things when it came to surviving. She'd understand you need to heal. She'd understand that I am made a certain way and that we have reached a compromise.... *Want* you?" He lifted an eyebrow, his black eyes challenging her. "We'll know differently, won't we?"

She looked away out into the bright January sun-

light, to Mr. Collier carefully helping his pregnant
forty-year-old wife across street. The child was their
first and both were glowing.

Gabriel was right; she wasn't ready to face life just
yet, to see Gwyneth's body rounding with a baby. At
times, Miranda's grief slipped beyond her tethers and
revealed more than she wished. Tanner was too careful not to speak of his joy and hurt her. Michael and
Kylie were bursting with excitement, quickly shielded
when Miranda was near—she expected that they had
their own news of a baby and the ache within her
grew. She couldn't bear casting a shadow upon her
brother's and sister's happiness. She couldn't bear living in her mother's empty house.

"Only for a time, Miranda. Until you feel better."

She rubbed her throbbing headache. Every part of
her now wanted to agree to Gabriel's offer, to take
shelter away from everything. "You're pushing me,
and I don't like it."

"The offer is mine. The choice is yours." Gabriel
looked away as if they weren't discussing the deep
traditions of Freedom Valley, where a man declared
his intentions in front of the Women's Council.

Miranda traced the rim of her water glass. "I'm in
pieces," she said finally. "Not at all like myself, and
you know it."

He nodded solemnly, those straight black lashes
shielding his gaze. The sunlight passing through the
window caught the dark tone of his skin, the angle of
his high cheekbones. He seemed timeless as the
mountains, his aura that of a man who spent his life
outdoors amid the pine and clear water. "I think that

your heart is wounded and that you are tired. You will be strong again."

Long moments passed and then Miranda gave way to the need running within her to escape. "Okay," she whispered bleakly. "I'd like to get away from everything for a while, and if it's necessary for you to present this deception—a trial marriage—I guess that's okay."

The smile lurking around his lips matched the tone of his deep voice. "Ah, the gracious acceptance of the doomed. Do you think you can ride in another week?"

"I don't feel like—" Then she caught that hard, straight look. The Deerhorns obeyed their own traditions. "You're coming for me in the old way, aren't you?"

"Yes. It is important to me. But if you prefer—"

"What am I worth?" she couldn't help asking, slightly surprised by her own humor.

He shrugged, a gesture that said little and yet everything. That black gaze slid down her gray sweater, woolen slacks and boots. "You're scrawny. Two horses maybe. Not my best ones."

She smiled at that. Gabriel used to tease her in the same way. "You'll get them back. This is only for a time."

He was trying to help her, but there were concessions to Gabriel's traditional-based honor. "I'll manage. Thank you, Gabriel."

At the cash register, Willa glared at him and stared pointedly at a jar filled with wrapped roses. Gabriel nodded and selected a tiny perfect yellow bloom.

While Willa watched approvingly, he tore off the long stem and slid the rose into Miranda's hair.

His hand rested warm and hard and callused against her cheek. She wondered why his gaze was so soft and seeking on her; she wondered why it called forth a tenderness she hadn't expected.

She wondered why, at times, he spoke to her in that careful, proper way, his deep voice curling intimately around her.

Later, she would see that Gabriel had not taken the baby blanket, and her senses told her that he was uneasy with returned gifts, especially gifts between women.

In his way, Gabriel was a very traditional man. He was also known to be very private, and Miranda knew it was no light matter for him to open his home to her.

A week later, the blinding morning sun danced across the crust of the snow. Tethered behind him, Gabriel's six best Appaloosa snorted steam into the frigid air. Three horses were his offering for Miranda; the one with the saddle was for her, one was to act as a pack horse, and another for him to ride on the return journey. He glanced at his four-wheeler, parked and ready for use, but today he was bringing Miranda to his home and nothing but the old-fashioned way would settle his heart. He'd cleared the narrow winding road to his home with the blade attached to his vehicle, because he wanted Miranda's journey to be safe. "As the crow flies," his home was not far from Anna's, yet it was over ten road miles. Intermittent horseback trails, passing through woods that a vehicle could not maneuver, closed the distance to five. Clumps of snow fell from the pines bordering the road to his mountain home, making muffled sounds as it hit. Branches cracked beneath the snow's weight and Gabriel's experienced eyes traced the paw prints of a big wolf, running alone and free. The wolves would mate for life and perhaps that was his nature, too, because he'd never wanted another woman. Chiding himself for the traditional ways that had always been within him, springing now to life, Gabriel led his best Appaloosa to Tanner and Gwyneth's ranch.

Miranda was right—he was pushing her. He was hungry for the sight of her, for the sound of her voice. When the wind stirred her hair, sending the blue-black silk swirling around her too pale face, Gabriel wondered about shaman's spells, for he was so enchanted. His hand gripped the saddlehorn and he realized that he had never been nervous of a woman before, except teenage Miranda.

Two days ago, Fidelity Moore's cane had hit the floor at the Women's Council meeting. Her high-pitched voice had run above the women's gossiping. "I want to hear what the boy has to say for himself. You've come here with Tanner Bennett, Miranda's brother, at your side. He approves of the situation? That you've finally decided to do right by Miranda? Well, speak, Mr. Gabriel Deerhorn. It is no light matter to ask for a bride before this Council. We want assurances that you are a rightful candidate for Miranda's future husband. Speak.''

In the bright January morning, Gabriel glanced at the cows mulling around the huge round bail of hay in the field. Freedom Valley was warmer than his mountain ranch, and his horses—except for the six with him—were staying at his father's place.

He thought of the women's faces, the Council earnest and fiercely protective of Anna's eldest daughter. Uncomfortable with opening his heart, he had spoken truthfully, simply. When he'd finished, he did not understand why the women's eyes shimmered with tears or why they hugged him. It had been no easy matter to tear away the shields of his heart, to speak to the women. Before he spoke, they had lashed at him for not courting Miranda, for giving her his child without wedlock. Yet as he'd finished, they listened intently. The words were true—how he had waited for Miranda to come back to him, how he would cherish her and make her safe, how she filled his life and that the years without her had been too empty. He'd been approved and the week of preparing his house for a woman startled Gabriel—the furnishings were plain and serviceable and probably not appealing to a woman.

At nineteen, he'd cut the timber for his log home, furiously planing it with his stormy emotions, his anger at himself for hurting Miranda. He'd tried to concentrate on the building of the cabin, not on the college girl who had taken part of his heart. He'd worked with ranchers until he dropped, then pushed himself home and worked more, so that he wouldn't dream of her, wouldn't miss her, wouldn't think of her sharing his home.

The newspaper had listed the college's honor students and Gabriel took pride in Miranda's achievements. But pride was little comfort when he ached for that slanted, mysterious green look as she considered him, the warmth of her body against his. He was a dreamer, of course, longing for what was not meant for him.

And now he had to protect her as she fought against life's hardships.

Did she still love the man who was no man?—the father of her lost baby.

Gabriel rubbed his leather glove over his chest, unfamiliar with the tightness there, the uncertainty of how Miranda-the-woman would greet him, and if she would like his home. *Would she stay? Would her lover come for her?* It was only because of his past with Miranda, he told himself. It was only because Anna's daughter needed his protection that he would take her to his home.

A hawk soared high in the sky as Gabriel told himself that he would protect his heart. Could he? Could he remain detached, unhurt when Miranda left once more? But then, how could he protect his heart against Miranda?

Tanner took the horses solemnly and handed Gabriel a small, soft thermal basket. "Gwyneth's warm milk and hot stew for the trip. When this is over— and I hope it works because Miranda is tearing the life out of herself—the horses are yours again. You're a man who keeps his traditions. I know this bridal price is important to you, even in this sham to help Miranda. Take care of my sister," Tanner said as, heavily clad in a long quilted coat, Gwyneth came to loop her arm around him.

"I will honor and treasure her, just as I told the Women's Council." Gabriel nodded and changed his saddle to another horse, swinging up on it. He reined the fresh horse toward the field separating Tanner and Gwyneth's land from Anna's.

Gabriel had barely tethered the horses when Miranda came from the house. "I'm ready," she said, as Gabriel took her small suitcase from her.

Dressed in a red down coat with thick insulated pants and winter boots, she looked like a child, her eyes shadowed beneath the red knit cap. She seemed too vulnerable and he'd taken advantage of her— Gabriel didn't like the panic surging through him, and tightened his lips to avoid saying too much. Miranda studied him. "What is it? Have you changed your mind?"

Gabriel nodded to the extra horses, one with an empty saddle, the other with a small canvas pack and dragging two long poles. He was suddenly nervous of her, afraid that she would turn away from his simple life. He had not exposed himself to another woman and he wasn't certain how to handle his fear that she might still reject him—his plan. "Does it look like it?"

His words were too sharp in the crisp freezing air and he tried to soften the impact. "You should take something of your mother's home, Miranda."

She shook her head and Gabriel eased that enticing wisp of black hair back from her cheek. The need to hold her close and soft ruled him, but she loved another man, defended a man who ran from marriage and children. Pushing away the thought, he concerned himself now only with Miranda's recovery. Then he moved into the house, wanting some of Anna's gentleness to help his barren home. He quickly folded a crocheted afghan from the couch, and moved into Miranda's feminine room.

When he returned, her arms were tight around his horse, her face pressed to the warmth. Gabriel ached to hold her, to warm her, but placing his arms around her would be too much of a declaration and he couldn't trust his heart—or his anger—then. What man could not want her as she carried his child, a beautiful gift? Why would he not want to give her his name?

She shook her head at the hope chest he carried, the afghan and Anna's daintily stitched patchwork quilt tucked beneath his chin.

"You would come to me without Freedom Valley's required hope chest?" he asked teasing her just a little to lessen the tension. When the familiar shadow crossed her expression, he added, "I removed the baby things."

"We can't take all that." When the *travois,* quickly fashioned by the two long poles behind the horse and wrapped in canvas was finished, she said, "I guess we can."

Two hours later, Gabriel swung down from his horse and walked back to Miranda. Through her sunglasses, used to cut the blinding glare of the sun on the snow, his expression was grim. "You are tired. This is too much for you. My tradition costs you. I was foolish in my honor and pride."

"I'm fine. You've been moving more slowly than you probably would without me. I know you're trying to be very careful of my...weakened condition. But I'm enjoying—" Miranda held her breath as Gabriel reached for her and swung her into his arms. He carried her back to his horse and carefully placed her sideways on the saddle. He tucked her long quilted coat around her legs, then swung up behind her. Gabriel's arms were around her, tugging her back against him, arranging her coat's hood over her knitted cap.

Drained by the day and her emotions, she closed her eyes and gave way to the warmth of his throat against her face, the familiar scents of a boy who had become a man. Snug and warm against him, she gave way to her memories of Gabriel—fishing, laughing, teasing her as Tanner's little "tagalong" sister. At sixteen, she'd had her crush on Michael Cusack, Kylie's new husband, or rather Michael's powerful motorcycle. Then Gabriel had given her wildflowers—

"I can't even remember what Scott looks like," she whispered suddenly, startling herself. Gabriel's body tensed, and against her cheek, his chest did not rise and fall for just that moment. She glanced up at him and found his grim expression, that flat, closed-in look. But she could feel his anger vibrating around her. "Scott was weak, not bad, Gabriel. He was as surprised as I was to find that he couldn't bear the thought of children, or marriage."

Gabriel looked off into the woods. A muscle crossing his jaw contracted and released. His next words were a statement, not an accusation. "He suited you. You lived with him."

"I'm thirty-five now, Gabriel. I wanted a home and children. I seemed so buried in my career and working overtime, that there was no time for anything else. I made time for a life and Scott had come from the same family-oriented background as myself. When

Mother died, something happened inside me and I wanted a baby, a little part of her to carry on. Until then, my thoughts of children and a family were only passing—one of those 'some days.' My biological ticking clock started in fast forward—I can't explain it, really. It just happened and I was terribly happy. But until then, Scott seemed to be a logical choice.''

''Ah. The statistical analysis of backgrounds for the selection of a mate.''

Miranda sat up, away from his strength. The blinding harsh light was no worse than her realization of how smug she'd been, how certain and clinical. ''You're mocking me. Isn't that what you did all those years ago? Decided that statistics were against us?''

She hated lashing out at him; it wasn't like her to dredge up the past, to wallow in it, but the old anger and frustration burst into the dapple sunlight.

Gabriel's hard mouth softened slightly. ''You feel like fighting? That's good. I've been worried that you'd lost your bristles. You're not going to slap me again, are you?''

The image of teenage Miranda hurled through the adult woman. She'd been hurt and blinded by tears at Gabriel's choice to separate, striking out at him. Tall and lanky, already packing on muscle from hard ranch work, he'd stood under her mother's backyard tree. The summer night had been sweet around them as he accepted her verbal blows and then the final hard slap to his face.

''Snob,'' the adult Miranda muttered now. ''You could have gone to college with me. That 'our life paths are different' stuff was just because you didn't want to try.''

"Could be. That was a long time ago. Now shut up and get some rest," he murmured easily, tugging her back against him. His chin fitted over her head and his arm curled securely around her again.

"You're wallowing in this big macho protective male role, aren't you?"

"And you like the last word, don't you?"

Miranda caught his gentle tone and asked, "Are we going to get along, tearing at each other?"

"Sure. You need to tear at something, don't you? It might as well be me." He nodded at the bark torn away from a tree. "Bear."

Gabriel was right. She didn't like her weakness, her vulnerability, nor her uncertain mood now, and she didn't like the dark anger stirring in her. The bear had only marked his territory, yet Miranda wanted to claw and fight and forget. "I don't know what I need. I don't want to feel anything for a long time...."

At four o'clock in the afternoon, the mountain evening crept over the snow, tinting it a soft blue. Made of rock and logs, Gabriel's home nestled in the pines, the windows looking like square mirrors, gleaming in the shadows. The huge barn was weathered gray, the metal roof showing reddish streaks of rust. In the sweep of a snow-covered field, the mountain's shadows and the forests, the colors blended soothingly. Gabriel swung down from the horse and again lifted Miranda, carrying her to his front porch. He placed her to her feet as he opened the door and a dark furry shape hurled itself past them, barreling down the wooden steps and into the snow. The gray striped cat stopped and daintily shook its paws, trying to rid itself of the snow. Gabriel's grunt was of pure disgust and he hurried after the cat as it leaped across the crusted snow. The man's weight, breaking through the snow made his progress slower, but soon Gabriel was scooping up the cat and tucking it against him. She hissed and clawed at him, not a fierce objection, but enough to let him know she wasn't happy.

Miranda hid her smile in her collar, as clearly nettled, Gabriel tromped up the porch's steps. He shoved open the door and lightly tossed the cat into the house. "She's mad at me for leaving her. Meet Jessica."

Jessica was too busy for pleasantries, tearing across the wood and cushion furniture and hiding in a stalking position. Gabriel scowled as the cat tore across the room again. "She'll get over it. I'll up her sardine ration for a few days."

He closed the door and began stoking the banked coals in the big, freestanding heating stove. Miranda noted his tense, dark expression, one he used when closing himself in, and she wondered why he needed to protect himself, what emotions could be troubling him. The house was spacious and filled with the scent of sage. Braids of sweet grass and camas bulbs hung from pegs, a basket of small bundles of sage for burning and purification sat on a high ledge. At his grandmother, White Fawn's home, Miranda had seen the elk horn, used by women to dig camas bulbs.

It seemed like another century since Juanita had brought Miranda to White Fawn's death bed, and the old woman's shaking, work-gnarled hands had

framed her face. Anna had spent many hours with
White Fawn, sipping tea in the makeshift outdoor
kitchen; as children, the Bennetts had sat upon White
Fawn's lap and enjoyed her stories. Approaching
death, the woman's face was dark and lined, but her
eyes still bright as she studied Miranda. "A good
face. Strong. Smart. She will become a woman who
will fight for what is in her heart. She is a warrior
with the need to test herself, too."

Jessica sauntered across the thick braided rug covering the wooden floors to her master; she rubbed up
against him sensuously. As if claiming her exclusive
territory, her yellow eyes found and locked on the
feminine intruder. She rolled over on her stomach,
and without pausing in his fire-building, Gabriel
reached to scratch her belly. He glanced at Miranda.
"Keep your coat on. The house will be warm soon."

The kitchen was at one end of the living room,
separated by a sturdy wooden table and two chairs.
Gabriel disappeared into a small side room off the
kitchen and a motor began to purr. He lifted the tap
of a plastic water container and filled a teakettle, placing it on the kitchen's gas stove. He began turning on
lights, exposing the simplicity of his home. The wide
wooden flooring planks had been varnished, a braided
round rug placed in the living room. The couch was
wood frame with dark brown woven cushions, matching those of a big wooden oak lawn chair. One of
Gwyneth's pottery mugs sat on the wide wooden
arms, and a low flat table clearly served as a footrest.
A table stacked with magazines completed the chair's
comfort.

Bending to the floor, Gabriel picked up a pottery

lamp—one of Gwyneth's—as if he were used to Jessica's antics. He ran his hands over it, checking for damage before straightening the shade. "Break this and you're out of sardines for a century," he noted darkly to the cat and moved to open the two bedroom doors. Jessica ran after him, tail held high, twining around his legs as if the sardine threat had hit home. "Won't work," he said to her, then looked at Miranda. "Open doors let the heat into the bedrooms. The stove provides the only good heat, but I keep a small heater in the bathroom to keep the fixtures from freezing. Oh, yes, no outhouse for me. I'm spoiled. You'll have to sleep with the door open or freeze." He nodded toward one bedroom. "The guest room. Look around. I'll see to the horses."

Miranda stood very still, feeling as if she were caught between the past and the future. She didn't feel a part of either world. The white chinked lines between the logs ran around her, yet she was somewhere else, not herself. The rough wooden beams overhead supported the ceiling, everything had a purpose and place in Gabriel's home. Once she'd known her purpose, known that she'd had to succeed and now she wasn't certain of anything—except she couldn't go backward.

Bookshelves lined one wall, brimming with books and magazines. A line of small, unmatched picture frames ran across one shelf and Miranda moved closer. There was the Bachelor Club, boys now grown into men. Her mother and Gabriel stood close, arms around each other. The picture had been taken within the past few years, her mother's expression one of peace and warmth. Gabriel's mother and father posed with their son and daughter. Juanita was petite with curling bright red hair and a pale face that had to be protected from the sun with a straw hat. Her husband, Carl, towered over her, angular and lean, long jeaned legs braced upon the land he loved. He stood hip-shot, the same knife-edge cheekbones as Gabriel, that fiercely proud look of a father with his family around him. Gabriel wore a boyish grin and Clarissa, his much younger sister, rode her father's hip. Always serious, Clarissa stared at the camera from behind her large glasses with the same flat expression Gabriel used to shield his emotions.

Resting across deer horns was a capture rifle used to tranquilize animals. The small, high shelf beside it contained a well-worn book of dosages and several vials, marked with chemical names, laid in a box. Tanner had told Miranda that Gabriel tracked potentially dangerous animals, or predators who had taken stock from the ranchers, helping the wildlife officials transport or terminate them. The knife in the fringed leather sheath was big and terrifying, and no doubt Gabriel was good with it. It was at odds with the colorful bottles of beads and leather crafting goods in a large shallow basket.

That array contrasted her life, filled with laptops, mainframes, conferences, company tension and corporate intrigue. In comparison to her life, long hours of overtime, stress and company deadlines, Gabriel's solitary existence seemed so free and clean.

Miranda wandered to a bulletin board, cluttered with scenic and animal photographs. The close-ups focused on milkweed pods, the silk and seeds caught in the wind. She felt like that, tossed by the wind, letting everyone else make decisions for her. The empty pods reminded her of—

She forced her thoughts away from that too-open wound and looked at the other pictures, carelessly tacked to the board—cattails slightly bent in the wind, grass rippling like an ocean wave, a chickadee perched near blue juniper berries, mule deer in flight, soaring over a fallen log, butterflies on dandelions. Brilliant blue flowers dotted a high camas field where Gabriel's female ancestors had dug for the bulbs years before white settlers. A wide shot caught a herd of white-and-black spotted Appaloosa moving through the mottled shade of a trembling aspen clump. The white bark of the trees blended with the horses as they flowed across the picture. Another photo was that of contrast, of sunlight passing through trees, slanting onto a lush green meadow. The same pictures were on sheets torn from magazines, copies of paychecks carelessly tacked beside them. Gabriel's pictures seemed to focus on life in motion, until she noted the picture of a man, crumpled in death. Shots of footprints in the mud, the victim's wounds and body position were exact.

Gabriel's footsteps sounded outside, followed by the customary *thump-thump* of boots stomped to dislodge snow. He shouldered into the door, carrying her hope chest and found her in the shadows. "Where do you want this?"

She shrugged, wondering how she would know where to put the chest, when she didn't know her own life. He placed it beside the couch and nodded. "I needed an end table there."

"You're a photographer?"

He glanced at the pictures, eyes narrowing critically. "I try. Basically I take the shots and send the film to a friend who takes care of the cropping and sales—it works out for both of us. He visits when the weather is good. I do some forensic shots when needed."

"I see. So you guide, photograph, ranch a bit and occasionally put up needy guests."

"I buy feeder calves and sell them in the fall. It's a living."

Miranda inhaled slowly. She'd been so driven, punching computer keys for hours, steadily building her career. In comparison, her life seemed cold and as inflexible as steel, while the texture of Gabriel's consisted of color and warmth and fulfillment.

A moment later, Miranda followed Gabriel into the guest room. He placed her suitcase on the bed, not a match to the huge dresser. Gabriel drew back the covers of the bed and placed Miranda's patchwork quilt at the foot end. "Open your bed in the evening, letting some of the warmth into it. The flannel sheets are warmer, but if you like, there are cotton ones."

"Everyone is worried about me. They're making decisions for me," Miranda said, her tone hollow and echoing in the still room. She inhaled the sweet-grass scent, braids of it resting in the basket that was White Fawn's design. "What I need, what I want, how to care for myself."

"For now. You're a strong woman. You'll get better. Would you like a cup of tea while I fix supper?"

She turned to him, wondering how he could know so much. Images flipped through her again—Scott's disbelieving, then angry expression, teenage Gabriel handing her the wildflower bouquet, White Fawn's bright, penetrating stare, her mother's funeral, the empty house, her empty body, the tiny body of her baby.... "Why am I here?"

His hand was warm upon her cheek, his thumb cruising along it gently. "To rest. To heal. It's no more than what other people have done and no less. I can take you back anytime you want."

"I didn't love Scott," she said quietly as he drew off her coat. "I settled for less. I simply made up my mind to go with my damned biological ticking clock. That's how I do everything—just make up my mind and do it. I was really wrong that time."

"You'll work it out. You're a woman, not a machine. You simply followed your heart," Gabriel whispered unevenly and for just a moment, his hands tightened on her upper arms, warm and strong through her sweater.

The eerie howl at the front door preceded Gabriel's dark tone. "That's Fletcher. He followed us up the road and he's been waiting until you leave. Clarissa is the only woman to come up here alone."

When Gabriel opened the door, a huge dog—a blend of German shepherd and wolf—entered warily. He padded to the heating stove and plopped down, yellow eyes gleaming. "Fletcher, meet Miranda. She's going to stay with us for a while."

Jessica, who had been napping, curled on the couch, hopped down. She arched and yawned and padded to Fletcher, snuggling up beside him. "Are you frightened of him?" Gabriel asked as Miranda studied the sight.

She shook her head, suddenly feeling too tired to move. "No. They adore you, don't they?"

Gabriel snorted. "I feed them. We understand each other." Then he looked down at her tears, skimming one away on his fingertip. "You're just tired, Miranda. You'll be fine."

Would she ever be "fine"? Right now, she felt as if pieces of her were scattered on the varnished floorboards and none of them fit. "Sure I will," she said, and prayed that somehow all of this pain would make sense.

Four

Healing can be painful, but it is a passage that must be made if one is to be whole.

Anna Bennett's Journal

Did Miranda think of her lover? *Did she still want him, the man who would not marry her?* Gabriel wondered darkly. He didn't trust the temper brewing within him, the stormy emotions. At midnight, Miranda slept restlessly in the next room. Lying dressed only in his jeans, his arms behind his head, Gabriel studied the firelight dancing on the rough wood beams of his room. He'd pushed her too hard, and now guilt and an unfamiliar jealousy rode him. When he'd held her on the ride back, she'd seemed so fragile and light, almost as if the wind would blow her away. Her spirit was wounded now, her face haunted, the fine bones showing too clearly beneath her too-pale skin. She looked like a ghost of the Miranda who had danced with him at Kylie's wedding. He wanted to go to her, to hold her close and safe. He listened for each sound, his body tense.

Her scent filled his senses, her bathroom toiletries dainty beside his few necessary ones. Tonight, taking a shower after hers, the feminine scents had startled him, curling around him. Those damp footprints on the bathroom rug were narrow and small when he placed his naked foot beside them. He'd stood in the small enclosure, breathing unsteadily, unprepared for the sensual need ripping through him. At first he thought the impact was a ghost of his teenage need, but the force was too great and too deep, hardening him.

Now he wasn't prepared for the sight of Miranda, dressed in flannel pajamas and a worn, long flannel robe appearing at his doorway. "I'm awake," he said, thinking how small and vulnerable she looked with the back light washing over her, wedging between her bare feet. He could hold one in the length of his open hand, his fingers could easily overlap her wrists.

Her arms came protectively around her body, the firelight glowing around her black hair. "I've got to get out of this depression, Gabriel. I have to."

"I know. You will."

"You're so certain of everything. How can you know?"

"I know you."

There was a moment's too-still silence and then Miranda erupted. Her temper licked suddenly, furiously at him. "Damn you. You always know everything, don't you? You always know exactly what is right. How wonderful that must be.''

He was pleased at that, because Miranda was a strong woman who was beginning to feel, to free her blocked emotions. Her robe fluttered behind her as she pivoted and stalked to her room, slamming the door behind her.

"You'll freeze if you leave that door shut," he called after her, not understanding her tumultuous mood, but appreciating the fire in it.

When the door didn't open, Gabriel shook his head. Miranda had always been an independent child and now she was a stubborn woman. He rose to his feet, padding to the closed room. He knocked on the door. "Miranda?"

"It's cold in here," she returned sharply.

He smiled at that; independent and stubborn behavior had its place, but not in a house with one heating stove. The small bathroom heater, used to keep the insulated pipes from freezing, wouldn't help the guest room. "Told you."

The bed creaked and then Miranda jerked open the door, glaring up at him. The fragrance of her hair and skin curled around him, unsettling in his masculine house, as she asked, "Why didn't you ever marry?"

He'd been relaxing a bit, the flash of fire telling him that Miranda was fighting to reclaim herself. Her fierce scowl tore through his safety; he wasn't prepared for that attack. He couldn't tell her that she was still the woman of his heart, that she would always be. "You should marry and have children, Gabriel," Miranda said firmly. "You're a man meant to have a family, to care for them."

He frowned down at her, not shielding his irritation. Who was she to tell him what he should do with women—when she was the only woman he'd ever wanted.

"Most women don't like it here. They say they do to please their boyfriends and husbands. No shops, no girlfriend chitchat. Too much quiet. Too many animals and itchy, yucky grass." He tossed her a challenge, to test the midnight fire and truth between them. "You'll want to leave, too."

Her finger jabbed his chest. "You don't think I can last, do you?"

"Not really," he lied, pushing her, enjoying life stirring into her.

With a toss of her head, Miranda padded back to bed. She climbed in and sat studying him, her head held in her hands. Jessica leaped up into her lap. Fletcher whined at the side of the bed until she reached to pet him. Clearly Fletcher had lost his wariness of women.

Gabriel leaned against the door frame, studying the sight of Miranda in bed, petting his cat and dog.

Miranda scooted down the bed and patted an empty place for Fletcher. The huge dog, weighing more than Miranda, accepted the invitation easily, plopping down and settling his muzzle over her legs. There was one thing missing in Miranda's bed—himself, Gabriel decided uneasily. "Gabriel? Thank you for bringing me here."

He nodded and turned away, his heart aching to hold her.

A week went by quickly and January became February, one month had lapsed since she'd lost her baby.

Drained by the past months, Miranda settled into Gabriel's home. With Fletcher and Jessica in her bed, warming her, the comfort of life nearby, she slept heavily. When she awoke, Gabriel was always there, his house warm and usually scented of food. Gabriel spoke little, but his presence was comforting. The steady rhythm of the day—his voice in the morning, talking with his animals, the meals they shared—began to soothe and relax her. He was usually gone in the late mornings until the shadows began to crawl over the meadow, but she could see him work with his three horses, feeding them, walking with them. At night, with his animals warm against her, she heard him prowling in the house. More than once, he'd come to her open doorway, a big man, his broad shoulders gleaming in the lamplight.

That old tightness rose, surprising her in a demand. She wanted him to hold her, to wrap her arms around that strong body and see if his kiss—edgy with hunger and sweet with tenderness—tasted the same. She'd fought the need to touch that hard jaw, to skim her fingers over those sleek black brows and ease the creases at the sides of his mouth. Gabriel was only trying to help, and she couldn't focus on the past, or transfer her body's needs so soon to another man. Miranda tried to push away the startling sensuality. She hadn't considered herself to be a sensual woman, but Gabriel was definitely filling her senses. Too masculine to be denied, his presence created unpredictable needs in her healing body.

This morning was bright and Miranda awoke to the scent of freshly baked biscuits. Gabriel and Fletcher

had already gone, and she had the house to herself—
except for Jessica who lay sleeping on the couch.

Miranda had enough of sleeping. She forced herself
to dress in jeans, a sweatshirt and socks. Bracing herself, she sat her morning cup of tea on the floor beside
her hope chest. Gabriel had taken more than the chest
from her mother's house. Inside were her mother's
crochet basket, that hook stuck through the loop of
thread, sunk into the spool, as if waiting for completion. The doily was delicate, a pattern Anna had long
ago tried to teach Miranda. Colorful lengths of embroidery floss, needles, and a small metal hoop
seemed too familiar.

Firmly placing the basket aside, Miranda saw the
framed pictures of her family, also taken by Gabriel.
She was a part of them still and they a part of her,
and she stood to place the frames on the shelf next
to Gabriel's family. The box he'd placed in the chest
was filled with her old drawing pads and pencils and
then her teenage handwork and memories filled the
rest of the chest.

An hour later, Gabriel pushed into the house with
Fletcher, his boyish grin proof of their play. He
stopped and stared at Miranda in the kitchen. "What
are you doing?"

She licked the frosting from her finger. To accom-
plish anything now was to reclaim a small part of
herself. "Cooking. Baking a cake and making a cas-
serole for tonight."

He whipped off his knitted cap and jerked off his
jacket, sitting down on the chair to unlace his boots.
He placed them neatly beside hers. Everything about
Gabriel was studied and concise, very controlled. One

dark look seared the house, her family pictures near
his, the afghan folded on the couch, his box of patch-
ing thread and needles lying next to a pile of his jeans
and shirts. In the kitchen, his washer was chugging
away, working on a load of brown nubby curtains.
On the ironing board, a basket of rolled and dampened laundry waited. Then Gabriel's gaze traveled the
length of fishing line, strung near the heating stove
and draped with her panties and bras.

Sweeping his hands through his hair, Gabriel
frowned. "I don't want you to work."

He seemed too rawly masculine, the frigid air
clinging to him, his black hair rumpled and shaggy.
The worn, thick flannel shirt and jeans and his thermal
socks completed the picture. The frosting spatula
seemed to tremble in her hand—or was that the shaking of her heart? "You said to make myself at home.
I have to do something."

He crossed into the kitchen, towering over her. His
tone was low and commanding, and for the first time
a fierce anger leaped from him, trembling in the large
room. "You are doing something. You're healing.
That's enough. I don't want you cooking or cleaning
my house. Tell me what you want done and I will do
it."

"Grump," she said lightly and on impulse slashed
her finger through the frosting bowl and reached to
swipe it across his lips. They opened and caught her
fingertip, and a jolt of electricity skittered over her
skin. The lick of his tongue followed her finger as she
drew it away.

She tried to breathe and couldn't, her senses too
filled with Gabriel, the heat coming from him and

trembling, snagging her own body. She couldn't turn
away from that warm dark gaze, stunned by the intimacy of it. Then his head lowered and slanted and
his lips brushed hers. The taste was familiar, and yet
new and exciting. She stood very still, uncertain she
hadn't dreamed the kiss. Gabriel straightened, studying the heat moving up her cheeks. "Your cheeks are
turning pink, the color of a wild rose."

"We were compatible. Scott and I were friends,"
she said breathlessly, the haunting thought bursting
into words. She needed Gabriel to understand. With
him—the man who knew everything about her—parts
of her life unexpectedly erupted, needing explanation.
The absolute clarity startled her, and sprung from a
need to clear her mind aloud. Her emotions felt as if
they had been stored too long, passing through a narrow bottleneck where she dissected them ruthlessly.
Why was she shaking so badly, her pulse pounding
through her?

"But this is between you and me, isn't it?" he
underlined coolly.

But this is between you and me... Miranda slept
restlessly, too aware of Gabriel in the next room. The
next morning, dressed in a heavy woolen sweater and
jeans, he sat in his chair cleaning his camera lenses.
Whatever bothered him hummed violently in the
wood-smoke-scented air and bounced off the white
chinking layered between the logs. Almost palpable,
his tension ricocheted off the wooden beams, circling
her. The morning shadows caught his taut expression,
that rhythmic hardening of his jaw. He suddenly

launched himself to his feet and began packing his canvas camera bag. "I'm going out."

"Where?"

"To take some pictures." His usually liquid deep voice held a frustrated, ragged edge she hadn't known. He was impatient, hurrying now to be rid of her, just as he and her brother had done long ago.

"I want to go." Her demand startled her. She wanted to walk and feel the cold, see the glittering sunshine on the pristine snow.

His black eyes ripped down and then up her body. "I'm hiking on snowshoes. You're not up to it."

"Try me. I've been exercising and taking my vitamins. I'm tired of sleeping." Whatever her biorhythms had been, they were spiking now. It was as if she were coming out of hibernation. Miranda felt like layers of darkness were being peeled from her and she wanted to reach out for life. Nettling Gabriel had always been very enjoyable, seeing just how far she could push him. She recognized that dark gleam now, the taunting challenge of a younger, carefree Gabriel. She smiled up at him, feeling warm and young, as if the past had just dropped from her. "Just don't call me a 'tagalong.'"

The nickname brought a smile, so brief she wondered if she had imagined the warm humor in his eyes. There was that lingering look, Gabriel searching her face as if trying to see within her. *Why was her heart trembling and her body heating?*

An hour later, Miranda trudged behind him in the snowshoes he'd made smaller than his own. Strapped to her boots, they'd been his sister's. Gabriel had insisted on bundling her, until only her eyes were to be seen. She'd had to wear sunglasses, while Gabriel moved easily without the confinement of heavy clothing, his face hard and angular in the brilliant light. He seemed so strong, so complete within himself. He spoke little, but those quick penetrating glances back at her told of his concern. "You haven't taken many pictures," she said, breathing heavily and disliking her weakness.

The blinding snowscape swept around her, the air crisp and fresh as though the slate had been wiped clean. Miranda felt life stirring within her, the excitement of being freed from indoors into this bright new world. Despite the weakness of her body, she felt wonderful. Had it only been a month since she'd lost her baby? Was that life calling to her? Had she come so far?

Gabriel's black, glossy hair escaped his knitted cap, the shearling jacket's collar turned up at his throat. He pointed to a winter rabbit, bounding along the snow then huddling beneath brush, sending off a flock of snowbirds into flight. Then he turned, eased off his gloves and lifted his camera to frame her face.

Following an impulse, Miranda didn't hesitate. She reached for snow, formed a ball and hurled it at him. The pleasure came from her childhood, when Freedom Valley children built forts and battled each other with snowballs, most frequently girls against the boys. Gabriel lifted a shoulder, protecting his camera and the snowball glanced off. He packed his camera into the bag, shielding it with his back, which Miranda hit with another snowball. She hit him twice more as he back-walked to her.

Suddenly he turned, placed his snowshoe over hers,

trapping her immobile, and grinned boyishly. Miranda struggled to pull her snowshoes free and couldn't. Off balance, she grabbed for his coat and held him tightly; Gabriel reached to the snow-covered pine branch over her head and tugged. A tiny avalanche of snow fell on her. It was an old familiar game, played as teen-agers and Miranda laughed aloud. "That's not fair!"

Gabriel brushed the snow from her cap, propping her sunglasses over it. Then that quiet searching tenseness danced on the brilliant sunlight and he slowly tugged down the scarf protecting her face. Emotions tangled and warmed as he studied her. Then in an uncharacteristic show of affection for Gabriel Deerhorn, he bent to place his cheek against hers. Held in place by the magic of that brief endearment he'd given her long ago as she grieved for her father, Miranda couldn't breathe. She turned her head slightly, resting her face within the warmth of his throat and collar.

The moment was brief and treasured, glittering in her like the life she was beginning to feel.

He turned slightly toward her, just as she was mov-ing away and those deep dark eyes caught her reflec-tion, his breath warm on her face. "Miranda," he whispered so quietly the sound seemed to slip into the glittering day.

His lips were cool and firm against hers, the brush light as a feather before drawing away. Shaken by the kiss, Miranda stared up at him. Gabriel's expression was kind, that of a friend, nothing more. She released the timid smile, uncertain that she had tasted the hun-ger of long ago in that brief moment. Gabriel gently adjusted her shawl around her throat and lowered her sunglasses into place. Did she imagine the tenderness of his expression?

She reminded herself that he was only a friend, trying to help. She couldn't misread his caring actions. He'd always been her brother's friend, sometimes tormenting her. He was the teenage boyfriend she'd adored and later hated bitterly. He was the man who knew more of her life than anyone. "I don't want your sympathy," she stated quietly.

"You haven't got it."

"Maybe I'll stay up here forever, in this fairyland, and not face my life. That would serve you right for this idiotic plan."

"Think of how boring my life was, how much you can make me suffer and how much gossip we're stirring up." That old charming smile was there, that fascinating roguish tilt to his head. "Feeling better?"

He'd looked like that years ago when he'd asked her to trust him, to jump from the top of an embankment down into his arms. He'd held her tight and safe then, and her instincts said that he was just as safe now. "Yes, thanks. I needed to get out."

Her first visit to the large weathered barn was later that day. She hadn't wanted to intrude upon him more than necessary and accepted his absence as the time he needed away from sharing his home. A heavy-duty, battered farm pickup was parked inside, an aged tractor, a small hay baler, a plow and field mower. The barn smelled of hay, bales stacked in the loft above and on the north wall, buffering the penetrating cold wind.

Gabriel was moving around his horses, talking to them in the airy cold space. They nudged him for the

grain held in his hand, and he rubbed their ears. The
mottled Appaloosa coats shifted in the dim light,
churning slowly around the man standing tall and
proud amid them, his deep voice like liquid magic.
Gabriel seemed to be a part of them as those dark
eyes found her in the shadows. "They're missing the
rest of the herd. They're staying at my father's during
the winter. It's warmer at his ranch."

"Do you ever get lonely, Gabriel?" she asked,
wondering how being with him could be so natural
and yet new—except when those long slow appraisals
crossed too deep within her and she had to shield
herself against him.

He shook his head and glanced at the pigeons entering their barn coop. He'd explained they were car-
rier pigeons, used to carry messages for the teen
members of his extended family. "I have what I want
now."

There was that look, that "seeing inside her" look.
"What do you want, Miranda?"

As the pigeons cooed and settled for the night, she
considered her thoughts. "Peace, I think. Most of all,
peace. I hadn't realized how tired I was. Even before
I lost the baby."

"You're a strong woman. You're getting better."

She leaned against the mottled throat of the Appaloosa near her. "I know I can't afford a second
mistake like the first—assuming too much, wanting
something that just wasn't there, wasn't real. This
isn't real, either. It's only a resting place, for which
I'm grateful."

In Freedom Valley, Tanner's wife would be rounding with his child, due the first part of June. Kylie,

Miranda's sister, would likely be pregnant from her January honeymoon, because Kylie never waited for anything she wanted. Miranda had wanted her child to grow up within her family's love, the cousins playing together.... "I can't stay here forever, Gabriel. We'll have to call the Women's Council and tell them this isn't working out. Or better yet, we should just tell them the truth and be done with it."

"Can't. No phone. You're either here, or I'll take you back. The rest of it, you can handle as you wish. Your choice."

She studied him. At times, Gabriel could nudge her emotions, firing them. "You don't think I'm suited for this—the frontier lifestyle, do you?"

"Nope. Can't see you gardening or canning beans, or—"

"I did all that with Mother, when I lived at home."

His look was too innocent. "You're 'city' now."

"I haven't changed that much. Neither have you."

He didn't answer and she knew that he'd slid into that protective shield where she could not reach him. A shadow crossed his face before he turned away, walking to the pigeons and reaching for one. He untied the band from its leg and frowned. "My mother and father are coming one day soon."

Miranda hadn't wanted to see anyone and yet Juanita and Carl would want to visit with their son. "Do they know of our arrangement? How kind you've been to me?"

Gabriel cradled the gray bird against him, stroking its blue-green iridescent head. "They know."

She didn't trust the dark, ominous tone as if he were dreading the visit. She *knew* she was. The Deerhorns were likely to ask questions she might not want to answer.

Miranda had taken to studying her mother's doily, trying to finish it as though she were trying to see the pattern of her life. She'd begun drawing Celtic patterns, comparing the eternal winding and strength to the doily. The graceful movement of her hands, the way she concentrated on the designs, fascinated Gabriel. Miranda was working her way through her emotions and he had no right to touch her, to kiss her on the mountain. She'd seemed so fresh and young then, her face pink with cold and her eyes lighting with pleasure as she threw snowballs at him.

Give her the peace she needs, he thought and added a reminder to himself, *you have no right to think of holding her, kissing her.* Miranda seemed so soft and fragile; she would turn into smoke if he touched her. Yet she was real, the scent of her clung to him, haunted him. Did she still think of him? The man who had run from her?

During the evenings, she often sat on the floor, the firelight playing on her glossy hair. It shifted like a silky wave around her face as she leaned into her work. She looked up at him and smiled as though just remembering he was in the same room. It was enough, he told himself, even as he clenched his hands to keep from reaching for her.

She turned to him that night, saw what was within him before he could shield himself. "You're brooding again, Gabriel. Why?"

He shrugged and began cleaning his tackle box, one she had thoroughly messed when they went ice

fishing. He began straightening the fouled lines methodically as was his way, while he tried to place his
thoughts in neat order. With Miranda nearby, his
thinking wasn't that clear—it ran more to placing
himself over that smooth graceful body and kissing
that incredibly soft mouth. She still tasted sweet and
innocent as she had long ago. Now with her green
eyes dark and mysterious on him, the sharp clench of
desire hit him. He could not love her, tell her of his
heart, nor could he lie. Instead Gabriel left the cabin
and the seduction that was Miranda.

It was mid-February now and Miranda had slept
for the most part of that time. She seemed suddenly
restless, and when he returned to the house, he found
her on the floor, staring at the firelight. He watched
her from the shadows and Miranda turned to him in
one of those lightning quick moods that startled him.
"You really didn't think we were suited, did you?"

"No, I didn't. I thought you should have better."
He saw her again, a teenage girl with her future ahead
of her, colleges calling her, scholarships waiting.

"You broke my heart, Gabriel Deerhorn. That was
a terribly arrogant thing for you to do, to make my
decisions for me." Then while he was struggling for
words, she turned back to the firelight. Her words
came back to him, quiet and firm. "I'm a woman
now. Never do that again. Never take away my
choices."

Gabriel held very still, aware that the kitten was
showing her claws. He hadn't expected the sudden
attack, the fierceness of it. "I will try to be very careful of you," he said, meaning it.

"That's just it. You're very careful of me, tiptoeing

around any subject you think might upset me. What subjects upset you, Gabriel? Why do you lock so much inside yourself, your feelings? Do you think it's fair that you know so much of me, and I know so little of you?''

"This isn't about me," he stated cautiously.

"No, it's about me, isn't it?" she asked sharply, clearly set to battle with him.

Uncomfortable with the confrontation, Gabriel stared at her. He couldn't tell her of his heart, how much she pleasured him, just by living with him. He couldn't tell her how much he feared she would leave one day, and his life would be cold and empty again. Instead he rose and left the house.

Two days later, the sound of snowmobiles tore through the mountains' morning silence as Miranda and Gabriel were hiking. Feeding on her growing sense of reclaiming herself, Miranda had wanted to push her strength, building it. Gabriel wouldn't let her take the snowshoe hikes alone and they usually moved in silence, his long legs taking shorter strides to accommodate hers. "My parents," Gabriel announced in a nettled sound like a growl.

"I haven't seen anyone for weeks. I'm going to enjoy visiting with your parents," Miranda said. She had decided that the Deerhorns were sensitive people—they would not press for details.

"They weren't invited," Gabriel reminded her darkly.

"My future in-laws?" she teased, enjoying his frustrated mood. Usually silent and controlled and in-charge, Gabriel settled for a burning glare at her. She smiled brightly at him, enjoying his discomfort.

When they arrived at Gabriel's cabin, Juanita and Carl Deerhorn were already inside, the scent of brewing coffee filling the house. Carl was an older version of Gabriel, tall and lean and weathered. Gray threaded Juanita's dark red curls, her light complexion still bearing freckles from summer sunshine. Slightly rounded now, Juanita hugged her son warmly, then Miranda. Juanita ignored her son's frown and placed a cookie in his mouth. "Brought your favorite. Dad wanted to eat them on the way, but then what reason would I have to come visit my son, hmm?"

"Yes, what reason," Gabriel murmured, eyeing her warily. "No Clarissa? My nosy sister decided to stay at home?"

"You know your mother," Carl said. "I suppose the 'pigeon boys' sent you warning she wanted to come. Those teenagers love their message system."

"What could I do? Run? Hide? She'd find me. I'm a grown man now, and questions about my life aren't appreciated, especially when asked by a nosy sister." Gabriel's grumbling wasn't in anger, rather the sound of doom, as he reached for another cookie. He placed it between his teeth, lifted the plastic container of cookies and his coffee cup and eyed his father. In silent agreement that retreat was safer than arguing with Juanita, the men walked out the door.

"Stop grumbling. Clarissa loves you." Juanita looked around Gabriel's house, clearly noting the items marking Miranda's presence. "It looks like a home now. Not so barren. I see you're working your mother's crochet hook."

"I'm not very good. I miss her."

Juanita's slight Southern drawl softened. "I miss her, too. She was one of my best confidantes when Carl was battling marrying me. He had some notion that we didn't belong together—just as Cynthia Whitehall did not belong with his ancestor. I had to fight for him, though he is certain that he is responsible for our marriage. It's a battle we have often, and one that used to be ferocious in our early days. But I knew from the moment I saw that tough cowboy that he was mine. Don't tell anyone, but he cried when Gabriel and Clarissa were born—simply came apart with pride and happiness. I've never looked back to the arguments my family tossed at us, or the threats of being disinherited from my family. They mellowed with age, especially with their grandchildren on their laps. My parents absolutely doted on them, and Carl was eventually, albeit reluctantly, admitted to be a good husband and a match for me."

Juanita shook her head, her blue eyes softening as she spoke of her husband. "Oh, he was a hard case to break, and I knew that I was just the woman to match him. White Fawn would later tell me that she knew no other woman would do for him, once we'd met and tangled. Your mother listened to me cry and whine and plot to have that stiff-necked, arrogant cowboy. She would want you to go on, and do what you're doing—healing and getting strong. You've always been strong."

"Not now. I've made a lot of mistakes."

"Everyone has, but to put a life back together, to make it stronger, takes a special courage."

"Gabriel was kind enough to offer his home—"

"You think he thinks only of you? I think he's a little selfish, wanting you for himself. My son is very old-fashioned, it seems. To offer for you at the Women's Council, to protect you from gossip in his own fashion," Juanita said, her blue eyes warm with affection. She lifted the whistling teakettle to pour water into a crockery teapot. With experienced hands, she wrapped a dishcloth around it to keep it hot, letting it steep. "Little Miranda. Gabriel's little Miranda. That's how he used to speak of you when you were dating all those years ago, and now you're back."

Miranda took the mug of hot tea from Juanita. She didn't want to mislead his mother. "You know the circumstance. He's explained?"

Juanita turned slowly to her, her expression serious now. "Perhaps he should explain to you. About the woman who has his heart."

Outside, Gabriel's father leaned back against the log wall and said, "I see you cleared more of the pasture. The grass should be perfect for stock this year.... It's a good sound, the women talking. Peaceful, isn't it?"

He smiled, tilting his head closer to the door. "Listen. Your mother's voice has that sound—she's talking about me and how hardheaded I was, determined not to love her. I didn't think a lady, with her soft voice and dainty ways, could fit into a Montana rancher's life. We fought early on, before you came. But I think a woman has steel in her when she wants to change a man's mind and have her way. I was helpless against her."

Gabriel tossed the last of his cookie to Fletcher, who caught it in midair. A midwife, his mother would be talking to Miranda about her body and her moods. The silent weeping was the worst for Gabriel. "Miranda misses her baby. I cannot help her."

"Give her another one. She has always had your heart. You will not give me grandchildren, if not with her. My mother told me that on her deathbed. She was never wrong about such things."

Gabriel tried to dismiss the burn of jealousy. It wasn't his right. "She chose another man."

"Because you denied her. Her woman's time had come upon her, and she wanted a child. Nature puts that in them, the same as in men, who want their song to be carried on long after they are gone. Her mother's death turned Miranda's mind and body to life and how it must go on."

Gabriel shook his head. "She was so young and bright. I could not bear her looking at me years later, feeling trapped and angry that her song had been taken away from her too early."

"She is your vision. If you do nothing but dream of her, life can be long and empty." Carl inhaled the fresh, crisp air. He was silent as Juanita's lilting laughter carried out into the sunshine. "Listen to that. When I first heard that sound, I knew it would be the music of my heart. I knew that I could not be as noble as our ancestor who turned away from Cynthia Whitehall. But I tried."

Carl studied his son. "How long do you think you can keep her here without revealing yourself?"

Five

———

Most women can draw upon a strength men
know little about.

Anna Bennett's Journal

Gabriel didn't think; he acted. In the barn, with the
third week of February cold and misty, he placed
aside the cup of early-morning coffee Miranda had
brought to him. He threw the lariat he'd been re-
winding toward the loft above him, and the loop slid
smoothly around her. Her arms pinned at her sides,
Miranda stood on the loft above him, her broom in
hand. She frowned down at him and in a restricted
movement sent the broom across the boards. Bits of
straw fell into his face and he blew them away.

Above him now, tethered by his lariat, Miranda had
just served him a notice he didn't like. "What do you

mean, you invited the Women's Council on Bride Courting here—to my ranch?'' he asked very carefully.

The broom swished again, sending more straw bits onto his face. ''It's what they do, inspect how you're treating me and how we're getting along. I've been here almost a month now and that's time enough for us to get settled. Unless you want to call this whole thing off—cancel our supposed arrangement, or tell the truth about why I'm here, it's the custom that the Women's Council visits and inspects.''

Gabriel tried to ignore how her denim jacket had gapped over the lariat. A button slid open on her blue flannel shirt, revealing a beige lace bra. One look at her underwear drying on the shower curtain could wipe his thoughts clean. Now her lingerie was on her and all he could think of was taking it off, pressing his lips to the smooth flesh below. A man used to control, his lack of it where Miranda was concerned disturbed him. In the house this morning, the chill had hardened her nipples beneath the form-fitting thermal top. His mouth had dried instantly and he'd had to turn away to shield his hardening body. Then she'd bent over to take biscuits from the oven, and the curve of her hips... Her soft, feminine scent could distract him too easily, riveting him, blocking everything from his mind but the need to hold and touch her. Unused to his body's instant and obvious reaction to Miranda, the sensuous desire locked in his body, Gabriel was not a happy man. ''I'm not a side of beef for women to inspect. I'm up here for the peace and quiet, not to have women nosing all over my place.''

''Spoken like a true hermit. Pray for a blizzard

then, because I used one of your pigeons to get the message to your cousin, who called Fidelity Moore, president of the Women's Council. According to the returning pigeon, Fidelity accepts our invitation.''

"Our?" he underlined darkly. Still holding the lariat, Gabriel climbed up the wooden ladder to Miranda. He tugged her closer to him. "I asked you to leave the barn alone. It's enough that everything in the house is moved around so I can't find it.''

Oh, he knew how to find her well enough—that feminine scent haunted his senses every moment of the day. He'd been stunned at her "getting in shape" exercises, hurriedly excusing himself. Now, he listened at the house door for the music she used, rather than entering at will. That body-clenching exercise and leg lifts carried the impact of a thousand-watt jolt. He'd always controlled himself and his thoughts, but he wasn't certain he could keep his composure when he'd reached to steady her. She'd stood on the kitchen counter, dusting the ceiling beams and Gabriel had seen her lose her balance—his hand had shot straight to that round, soft bottom. The touch burned him, and he mumbled a quick excuse to exit the house for more wood. At night, he heard her stirring on her bed, and hot, sweet images flew into his mind, devastating him.

"Take this rope off me," Miranda ordered fiercely and with her arms tethered, swished the broom at him.

Gabriel held the lariat firmly, not enough to hurt her. He tilted her face up with his fingertip. "Now get this. You are going to cancel."

Fire shot into those green eyes, burning him. "This is all part of the deal, Gabriel. Take it or leave it. My mother treasured these women and the customs of this valley.''

He leaned down to her. ''You're getting awfully bossy lately. You must be feeling better. Have you sent a message to your lover as well? Did you change your mind about him? Is he coming for you?''

Gabriel cursed himself and his fears that Miranda would leave him, returning to the man who left her. Miranda's expression was blank for a moment, and then furious. ''You think I'd want him? *Take this rope off.*''

He shrugged, uneasy with revealing his jealousy into the barn's air. He hadn't been vulnerable, and emotions were tricky and slid from his keeping too easily now. He lifted the lariat from her and she flung herself at him, sending them tumbling back against the wall of hay bales. Gabriel turned, placing his hands on either side of her head. He didn't know how to handle her now, those green eyes lashing at him, her mouth tight with anger—

Her mouth…

Her anger slid into another emotion he could not define. Though they were not touching, he sensed that her body was less tense. She had that curious, soft look, tracing his features, looking too closely into the passion he would shield. With Miranda, he sensed that need would be tender and growing like forest tinder ignited by a lightning bolt.

There with the barn's cold air churning with the scent of horses and hay and leather, golden bits of dust swirling on the shaft of sunlight between them, Miranda slowly lifted her lips to his.

He held very still, fearing a movement would send

her away. Against his, her mouth was soft as a buttercup's glossy petal, tasting of curiosity and warmth. He inhaled her breath, took it into him, just as he wanted to make her a part of him, of his heart and soul, so that she could never leave him again.

"I'm sorry," she whispered breathlessly. Before she hurried away from him, Gabriel took her shy blush into his heart.

On the floor level, she turned, her legs braced apart and her fists curled tightly. She slowly looked up at him. "You were wrong, Gabriel. Admit it. Our paths could have been the same all those years ago."

"That time is ended," he said, uncertain of her now. What did that kiss mean? Did her heart beat as wildly as his?

"You just make certain that you look like a happily tended man when the committee arrives, Gabriel Deerhorn. They're coming next week. Work on a real glow, will you? Meanwhile, I'm going for a ride."

She walked toward the bridles and saddles and fear leaped into Gabriel. She still seemed too fragile and tired easily—if she hurt herself… *"Do not lift a saddle. If you want to go for a ride, I'll saddle the horses and ride with you."*

"No, thanks," she returned lightly, shoving open the barn door to enter the corral. Outlined in the brilliant sunlight, she turned to him again. "You're not invited and stop giving me orders. Don't forget that I was raised in this country, too, Gabriel, and I've saddled horses. I've ridden in snow…I'm smart enough to know that I shouldn't go too far when I have an afternoon appointment with the doctor. You're a snob in your own way, you know."

Snob. The word stopped him cold. That was the second time she'd labeled him with the unattractive name. He opened his mouth, then closed it, too aware that when Miranda chose to fight, she was very effective.

Hormones, Miranda thought late that evening as she sat next to Gabriel. The Jeep's headlamps shafted through the bluish shadows of the narrow road leading to his home. Gabriel was silent, as usual, a man who said little and yet who seemed to have a river of understanding inside him.

She wanted Gabriel to hold her, and to make love to her. This morning, she shouldn't have kissed Gabriel's hard, set mouth, reacting to her unsteady emotions. But just then, suddenly nothing had changed in all those years. He was still Gabriel, tall and strong and safe, and she still adored him. But the underlying current between them had shifted into a primitive beat she didn't understand. Or was that the heavy pounding of her heart? Was it her body changing, coming to life after trauma? Could she trust her emotions now? When she'd taken her lonely ride, she had been so angry with herself. Gabriel hadn't touched her, except in a friendly way. He'd given her no encouragement and yet every nerve in her told her to lift her lips to his and *feel.*

She looked out into the pines bordering the narrow, winding road. She hadn't felt for so long, life moving in fast motion after Scott left. She'd been consumed with making her future baby's life safe and now— A pine bough swished along the window, hissing against the glass. Her thoughts danced between a man whose face she couldn't remember, whose voice she couldn't remember, and the babies rounding Gwyneth's and Kylie's bodies.

In Freedom, Gabriel had made a point of squiring her to the Wagon Wheel for lunch and then to the doctor's office for her checkup. He'd paid for her bill, despite her hushed protest as the nurse looked on with interest. They'd shopped for groceries together and from obligation more than need, she'd visited with Gwyneth and Kylie. Kylie had just happily confirmed that her baby had been created on her January honeymoon. Miranda had tried to be natural, to show them that she felt only happiness for them, but she couldn't help feeling so utterly empty. Later, at her baby's grave, Gabriel had placed his arm around her.

They'd stopped at Anna's house and Gabriel had gathered the bulbs and clay pots and the flat window beds used to start tomato seedlings for her garden. The errand-day had exhausted her, new situations springing at her from every direction. Never far away, Gabriel was quiet as usual, those dark eyes quick to note her uneasiness. He seemed to steer her through the day, deflecting any hardships. At her mother's, she'd leaned her forehead against his shoulder in that old familiar way, using his strength as her anchor.

The flower bouquet Gabriel had purchased at the grocery store rattled within the paper sacks, the scent filling the Jeep's cab. He glanced at her, shifting easily into another gear over a small mound of snow. "Hard day, hmm?"

"Very hard."

"It will get easier."

"Will it?" she asked dully. "I feel as if I'm a robot winding down."

"You're shifting gears is all," Gabriel noted, scanning her face. "Getting ready for the rest of your life." He brushed the hair back from her cheek, his thumb circling her ear. The gesture seemed so intimate, far from sensual, and she leaned her face into his hand. When her lips brushed his palm, Gabriel's indrawn breath hissed through the small enclosure. His hand eased away, clenching the knob on the floor shift until his knuckles were white.

She shook her head. She'd made him uncomfortable, a man who ignored everything to help protect her from gossip. "I never should have involved you. This whole situation—"

"Is what I want."

"You should be role-playing the would-be husband for a woman you love." Miranda didn't like the thought of Gabriel loving another woman, as his mother had said. Yet Miranda had no right to be so curious, to want to know more about the woman he loved.

Gabriel was silent, his profile hard in the dim light. He inhaled roughly. "Is it a hardship, being with me? For only this short time while you heal?"

"It's the first real peace I've had in years," she said honestly, vehemently. "You must know that."

"When the ladies come, how much of a glow are you expecting me to produce?" he asked, reminding her of the happy-husband-to-be image she'd wanted. "A small glow? A medium glow? Or just plain sappy-in-love-with-you glow?"

She stared blankly at him, amazed at the ability he had to distract her.

"You're not going to cuddle against me, and maybe even kiss me when they're around, are you? Yuck." In the dim light, his boyish grin flashed at her.

She recovered enough to lightly punch his shoulder and return the grin. "I'm going to make you suffer just as much as I can. You're enjoying this whole thing, aren't you?"

"Sure. I need a little excitement in my old age. Get me a cookie from Eli's Bakery sack, will you? In the back seat?"

Miranda turned to reach for the cookies and her breast brushed Gabriel's shoulder. He seemed to tense, adjusting his body away from her, allowing her room to sift for Eli's Bakery sack. Was her body still so sensitive that the slight contact burned?

He'd withdrawn again, his expression tight as if he couldn't wait to get out of the Jeep and away from her. That muscle in his jaw contracted and released again as though some inner leash had been tested and denied. Whatever his dark moods were, she ached to step into them and stir them until the truth sprung free. She placed the cookie in his teeth and studied him. "Your mother said you loved a woman. Who is she? Won't she mind me living with you?"

He chewed slowly and took his time answering her. Gabriel's expression was closed, as if he were mulling his thoughts before expressing them. "My mother should keep her thoughts to herself.... The woman in my heart is kind and thinks of others before herself. She would protect them with all her being. She would understand that you need peace. That I have little to offer but that.''

"Where is she? Who is she?" She knew so little about him, while he knew intimate details she'd never told anyone but her family.

Again, there was that long, thoughtful silence. "She is always with me, close inside. But to see her, I go to the mountaintop and camp, waiting for her. She comes in the smoke and she's round with a baby—my baby. Everything that I am or will be lies with her. I have tried to be with other women and still she haunts me, her eyes soft in the smoke."

Miranda stared at him, shocked at the emotion in his deep voice. He had never revealed so much about his feelings. Gabriel's senses had always been tuned to his Native American heritage, and now he spoke of a vision, a dream woman. Miranda settled back in her seat, slightly jealous, ridiculously so, of a woman who was fantasy and smoke.

Later that night, Miranda studied herself in the cabin window's glass, the night freezing and yet damp outside. Then Gabriel's face loomed in the glass above hers, his stark image familiar and yet new. His body heat licked at her skin beneath her pajamas and robe.

She ached for him to touch her, trembled with the need.

He hadn't touched her in a way that said he felt anything for her, other than friendship. Maybe she wasn't— "Gabriel, do you think I'm...desirable?"

"I think a man would want you," he said very slowly, in that deep, liquid voice that curled intimately around her.

She turned to look up at him, to see if there was sensual hunger in those marvelous black eyes, but Gabriel had withdrawn behind his harsh, unreadable expression.

"So it's working out, then," Fidelity Moore said in her high chirpy voice. The last week of February's bright midmorning sunlight shafted into Gabriel's house as Fidelity scanned the mix of Gabriel's and Miranda's possessions. "Just as I knew it would. Your mother would be pleased that you are working with her crochet hook and embroidery hoop. She would have loved to know that you have planted seed in the kitchen window for garden plants, just as she always did. I thought highly of your mother, Miranda. She was a woman of strength and conscience, and not once complained of hard times. I see her in you. Only a strong woman would come back to find herself and her love."

She used her cane to walk to Miranda's bedroom and then to Gabriel's. Gabriel slashed a dark, irritated look down at Miranda as Fidelity said, "Neat as a pin and homey. A little plain, but then a woman needs time to make a home her own. Miranda is simply blooming, young man. You must be treating her well."

"Very well." Miranda glanced at Gabriel, who had stiffened as he stood beside her. A private man, he didn't like his life, nor his home, inspected, and now the Women's Council had invaded it. She leaned against him, to comfort him, because he looked like he'd escape at any moment. His hand went to her waist and then slid fractionally lower, fingers digging in slightly where the women couldn't see. He tugged her closer, fitting her against his lean body. The unfamiliar gesture from Gabriel surprised her.

Fidelity's bright blue eyes warned Miranda. "The boy has a tongue and he's spoken much about his dislike of women inhabiting his mountain retreat. Let him speak for himself and tell us why he accepts you and runs from all the other women chasing him."

Miranda hadn't thought of Gabriel running from anything, anyone. "Other women?"

"Of course, he's been evidently involved with you, visiting you in Seattle, or else you wouldn't have created a child together. You never should have skipped the customs that the Founding Mothers set up to protect and insure a good marriage, my dear. Coming to meet us outside, you two looked perfect together, 'like a good pulling team of horses,' my dear departed Alfonso, used to say."

"Tracked her down and impregnated her," Sadie McGinnis muttered indignantly. "Those Bachelor Club boys…"

Gabriel's smile was nothing less than a roguish smirk and Miranda nudged him with her elbow, tossing him a warning look. He lifted his eyebrows, looking bland and innocent. Dahlia Greer, an experienced and outright sensual woman with several deceased husbands, laughed outright.

Fidelity's stern look focused on Sadie, renowned for her open views on the Bachelor Club "impregnating" any and every available, vulnerable woman. Then Fidelity turned back to Gabriel. "I would have liked to have seen more courting. It is Miranda's option to invite and court you, you know. The Founding

Mothers wanted to make certain that women were active in selecting their future husbands. But with snow and this winding mountain road, I see the difficulty of her courting you. You have no problem with the isolation of Gabriel's home, the farm life, after your career in business, my dear?''

Gabriel tensed again, looking outside the window, pulling himself away from her. His hand eased away from her as if he didn't want to tether her. If there was anything that made Miranda want to claim him, to get his attention, it was *that look*.

On impulse, Miranda stood on tiptoe and kissed his cheek. ''He's nervous,'' she explained gently, delighting in riffling that cool, distant, totally arrogant look.

''We're taking our time working things out,'' Gabriel said smoothly, serving back a bit of her torment. ''But I wish she'd court me. A man should have some romance.''

''Mmm,'' Fidelity murmured thoughtfully. ''Yes, you should. Miranda, do not let it be said that you didn't court your man.''

''If she doesn't nab that gorgeous hunk of man, she doesn't deserve him,'' Dahlia noted.

''I didn't know I was so appealing, Ms. Greer,'' Gabriel returned in that soft, lilting tone, his smile devastating.

''Why, you are just absolutely delicious, Mr. Deerhorn,'' Dahlia returned at ease with the playful flirtation.

Miranda mentally shook her head trying to clear it. Gabriel had unexpected facets and when he wanted to, he dropped the silent leave-me-alone act and reached for the charm.

"I think that went well," Miranda said later, as she stacked the teacups into the sink. "I don't want any of them worrying about me. I couldn't have done this in my mother's home, but now that it's over—I think I can manage. We should talk about ending this, Gabriel, you have to go on with your life, and I have to go on with mine. I'm more comfortable with people now, and I'm going to take pleasure in the broods my brother and sister are creating. You've been so kind. However you want this handled, I will do my best to—"

"'Kind?'" The word cut at her, his expression fierce and angry, surprising her. "I'm checking on the horses," Gabriel stated curtly as though he couldn't wait to escape the house, echoing with the sounds of women's chatter. The sound said he'd had enough of women and of her—

Miranda turned to him and his look took her breath away, staking her hotly as if he wanted— She swallowed, her hands shaking so badly that she dropped the next cup into the dishwater. Gabriel had looked as if he'd wanted her desperately, as if he wanted to make love to her. The air hummed between them and she couldn't move. She wanted to undress, to have him undress her. To feel his lips against her skin... The silence rocked with a primitive sensual beat... and when the fire in the heating stove crackled, she jumped, because the image of his tall body, gleaming and powerful rising over hers had seemed so real. She'd never been looked at like that, as if a man could devour her, claim her, never let her go....

She was misreading him, of course. Her body was coming to life and receiving wrong impressions. Ga-

briel's actions had been kind and nothing more. He
was tense because of the earlier strain, his home invaded. She tried to keep her voice even, concealing
her uncertainty. "Yes, you'd better do that."

By late evening, Gabriel hadn't returned. Miranda
had prepared dinner, baked bread and had finally admitted she was afraid for him. He was an experienced
woodsman, but he'd never been late for dinner. Gabriel was a man who needed his privacy. Perhaps he
was using the forest to soothe him. A "chinook," a
warm winter wind, howled fiercely around the house,
a lonely sound like that of a lost soul. Perhaps it was
his "woman in the smoke" calling to him. Perhaps
he'd gone to see her.

Fletcher paced the house restlessly, whining and
looking at the door, evidently wanting to be freed. He
growled, his hackles raised. Once, he lifted his head
and an eerie howl that spoke of his wolf's blood iced
Miranda's skin, lifting the tiny hairs on her nape.

Leashing Fletcher, making certain he wouldn't tear
off into a possible wolf pack, Miranda made several
trips down to the barn. As restless as the dog, she
watched for Gabriel through the house's windows.
His tracks led off into the woods, following those of
a horse. On her last trek outside, she noted the big
cat's paw prints circling the barn and without exper-
tise, Miranda knew they were that of a mountain lion.
Fletcher continued pacing the room as if he sensed
Gabriel needed him. If Gabriel were hurt…if a mountain lion… Miranda hurried to make hot tea, pouring
it into a thermos. She settled the house, turned down
the damper in the heating stove and quickly bundled
for the freezing weather outside. With her snowshoes

lashed to her boots, food and a thermos in the back-pack, she released Fletcher out into the dim light, fol-lowing him with a flashlight. ''Go, boy! Find Ga-briel!''

Six

A dash of temper fuels strength and pride. It's good, sometimes I think, to take temper out of the drawer and let honesty clear the air. Miranda holds too much inside, but one day she'll fight for what she wants, leaving nothing unsaid or undone.

Anna Bennett's Journal

A clump of melting snow slid from a pine bough and plopped down beside Miranda. Fear ruling her, she jumped, the flashlight's beam searing off into the tall pines. Fifteen minutes ago, Fletcher had raced ahead, ignoring her call. She prayed that he had found Gabriel safe. She'd lost his tracks, but continued in the same direction.

An hour in the forest worrying about Gabriel

seemed like an eternity. She'd tied her snowshoes to her backpack; they were good for open country, but not for the forest's dense brush, catching on twigs. She fell, pushed herself up awkwardly and trudged on in the snow, the chinook's winds hurling around her.

The flashlight battery was dimming and finally there was nothing. Weary, terrified for Gabriel, Miranda threw it away and marched on, the shadows seeming to come alive. Her backpack, not that heavy at first, caused her shoulders to ache. In the night's distance, Fletcher barked furiously and then nothing.

She ran toward the sound, dragging breath into her aching lungs. The wind swooped at her, tearing away her woolen scarf as if Gabriel's woman didn't want him to be found.

From behind, something grabbed her coat, immobilizing her. Terror surged through her as she thought of the size of the mountain lion's paw prints. She turned, fists flying and a mitten glanced off Gabriel's face, just as he ordered roughly, "Hold still. Stop fighting."

Because he was Gabriel and she had been both terrified and angry, she hit him again, this time in the chest. He grunted, scowling down at her while Fletcher leaped and played and threw his one-hundred-plus pounds into a friendly bump against her legs. She struggled for balance and Gabriel's fist locked onto her jacket, just beneath her chin. He hauled her up close to him. "It's a hell of a night to be out for a stroll, lady," he said tightly.

She was still fighting terror, her reasoning shooting between it and anger and the need to throw her arms around him. "If you can, I can."

Gabriel raked off his knitted cap and shoved his hand through his hair. "Now that's a childish statement."

She had to know— *"Were you with her?"*

He shook his head and stared blankly at her. "Who? My mare? Yes, I was. She takes a notion to go off into the high meadow once in a while. I left a note in the barn."

Miranda thought back to how frightened she'd been for him, disregarding the paper tacked to the door. *"I was worried about you!"*

"You're tired and freezing and illogical. Did it ever occur to you that you might be that big cat's dinner?"

Gabriel's cool control only made her more angry and frustrated; she tossed fear away and the other two emotions swallowed her now, the chinook wind's howl rising eerily in the night, coursing through the trees and swishing the branches. "I'm trained for logic, remember?"

"You should have stayed put. You're not trained for night hunting in the mountains." Gabriel's leather glove eased her scarf away from her face. "You're in a snit, lady, and this is no time to debate whatever mood you're in now. You need a warm fire—"

She wrestled the backpack from her and hurled it at him. She'd come after him because Gabriel was all that mattered to her. Not because he might be in danger. Not because he had been so supportive, a strong anchor holding her in rough times, but because whatever she felt for him years ago was a shadow of her emotions now. While she stood, buffeted by fear and anger and tearing through layers of what was important in life and what wasn't, Gabriel seemed unaffected. '''Stayed put?' Like in not meeting life and whatever it holds? I won't let you do that to me, Gabriel.... That's a thermos of hot tea in that backpack. For you when you're lying half frozen down some ravine with one broken leg, and a mountain lion gnawing on the other and I'm tired of the subject always being 'what I need.'''

Gabriel closed his eyes and shook his head as if dealing with a child's tantrum. With apparent effort, he kept his uneven tone low. "The mountain lion had more sense. He's back in his den, keeping warm. His tracks veered off mine about a quarter mile back. When I saw Fletcher, I knew you'd—"

"Who do you think you're dealing with? Why can't you show me what I'm showing you? You're angry with me—well, tell me that. Don't—"

That dark flash of anger tore across her like a sword and she reveled in the reality of Gabriel stirring past his self-protective shields. Because her emotions were flying now, out there on the howling wind, Miranda released them full force. She threw her weight into the shove, both her hands on his chest. He didn't move, as unreachable as ever, no reaction. "It's always about me, isn't it, Gabriel? What about you? What is behind all those nice placid remarks, the encouragement, the little you have to say about yourself? Just once, I'd like to hear—"

Gabriel turned from her, shutting her away, and only infuriated her more. Miranda stamped back a distance from him, then turned and retraced her path in the melting snow until she could see his face clearly. She tore off the coat hood covering her knitted cap. "I hate that—when you shut me out and when you run from any situation. Well, you're not running from this one. You used to be so open with me—enough to tell me that 'our life paths are different.' Oh, you could do that well enough. What changed you?''

"It's cold out here," he said too coolly, too logically. "Maybe you could wait to have this tantrum or whatever back at the house."

She jabbed a mitten-covered finger into his heavy coat. Gabriel grunted, but he didn't move. He'd shoved that nick of anger behind his walls, and that knowledge hiked hers a notch higher. "Oh, no. You're not running from this one, buddy."

He smiled a little at that, watching her. "What would you do if I did? Track me down?"

Gabriel as a confident, indulging male, secure that he could protect her wasn't what she wanted. She wanted equal terms now, not patronization. "I did it once, I can do it again. Every time I get too close to a subject you don't want to discuss, you either throw the conversation toward me, or you're gone, tuning me out or running away."

"Miss me, did you? What is this? Some aftermath of staying in the house too long? Maybe you're right. Maybe you have certain rights to know more."

That magical deep lilt coursed through the howling wind, staking Miranda with its sensual tone. Then Gabriel's big hands were framing her face, drawing her lips up to his. Eyes wide-open, she watched his intent expression, the line deepen between his brows, his lashes close. At first his lips were cool and firm, then they opened and played and nibbled and...

Miranda sank into the sweet kiss, tossing away everything but the magic that was Gabriel, that had always been Gabriel. He eased off her knitted cap and his hands dived into her hair, fingers splayed open, holding her as he slanted his open mouth on hers, locking the fit. The heat and hunger tore away the sweet taste and hurled Miranda into her own shaking hunger. She put her arms around his shoulders, opened her lips to his and felt the primitive beat of his passion, tuned into it so strongly that it became her own, trapping her body, pounding at her. She met him out there on that stark plane where shields were ripped away, desire burning bright. His mouth cruised her face, the kisses hard and hot and welcome, tasting of dark nights and skin upon skin. Tasting of eternity and vows and—

Shaking with sensual need, unprepared for Gabriel's own, and with too many layers of bulky clothing between them, Miranda eased away from him. Passion had honed his angular, hard face, his eyes narrowed and sultry, and his mouth rich and soft with the kisses they'd shared. "What was that, Gabriel?" she asked very carefully, wanting to make certain she understood the velocity and heat of that kiss.

"I think it's pretty clear. I want you. I always have." The words didn't come easily...it was as if he'd torn them from his soul. He took a deep unsteady breath and pushed the truth through the howling winds. "*You're* my woman in the smoke."

His statement knocked her back against a sapling and she leaned against it for support, trying to put all the pieces of the puzzle together—trying to make sense of the years wasted between them. He'd just kissed her as if nothing could tear him away. She'd

absorbed the heat and impact of his desire, her own
body shaking now in reaction.

"What's the matter?" he asked unevenly, clearly
unsteady and wrapped in his own emotions. His angular face suddenly seemed so weary and sad, mixed
with a frustrated tenderness. He wasn't a man to dis-
play emotions, but suddenly the wind whirled them
around him. "Don't the statistics add up? I'm just as
unsuitable now as I was then, yet it hasn't changed
how much I want you. But I am a foolish man and
cannot help the dreams that come to me. Sometimes
I hunt them. The woman in the smoke is round with
child, Miranda. My child. What I am will go on with
that child, and what came before from my father and
his father before him. But that is not for you—my
mind tells me this, not my heart. You belong in another place, not with me."

"Let me get this straight," she whispered huskily
as she struggled for reality, sorting through every nu-
ance of his looks, his voice. "You still care?"

He looked at her darkly, a big male used to keeping
his distance, prodded into an admission he didn't like.
"We aren't a good match and you know it."

Miranda held to sorting the facts, keeping to the
facts. She focused on absolute clarity, not wanting
one false detail to interfere. "This isn't about careers,
or lifestyles, or money, is it? It's about a man and a
woman."

"Maybe." He nodded, tilting his head and watching her in that quiet assessing way.

"You coming after me, the bridal price—that was
real to you, wasn't it?"

He nodded again, and she continued working

through her shocking discovery. "You wanted me here, living with you."

This time a nod wouldn't do; his anger struck through the chinook's howling winds. "Do you have to drag everything out and tear it to pieces?"

"What did you expect to gain?"

"I wanted to give you shelter. I wanted to protect the woman who haunted me, day and night. The way you looked at Gwyneth, at the baby nestling in her— as if it were tearing you apart.... Then for more selfish reasons—I wanted a little bit of you, just a short time to hear your voice, to see you in my home, to smell the perfume of your body—"

"All those years," she murmured, anger simmering like hot coals about to burst into flame. "All those years lost when we could have had—"

"What? For how long before the world called to you? You're smart, Miranda. Your future—"

"Lies where? With a man who ran from responsibility? With my own delusions that I could make life work *my* way? *How dare you, Gabriel. How dare you make my decisions for me and not serve me the truth.* That's what all the silence is about, isn't it? Why you run from any situation that might be considered intimate? Why you don't come too near?"

Gabriel's hand swept through that rich, shaggy hair. Caught by the wind, it swirled around his face. "You're angry, and this isn't the place to discuss—"

"I'm very angry. You're still making decisions for me, big ones. You decide what's safe to talk about and what isn't. *You* decide what is a dangerous area and what isn't, where I should be, and what I should do after losing my baby. You're telling me that you fantasized about me—you wanted me all this time. *And I didn't know it? How was I supposed to know? You kept that from me?"*

"That's a stretch, and you know it. You were vulnerable, I agree. But I wanted to give you protection—" He frowned and closed his lips as Miranda's green eyes seared him.

"Well. This certainly has been an interesting, but a bit late, little discovery," she said briskly, before turning and walking away from him. Furious with Gabriel and herself for letting all those years escape, Miranda didn't want him to see her tears. *I want you. I always have.... You're my woman in the smoke,* he'd said. All those years they could have had...

"Ride the horse. You're exhausted." Gabriel frowned at the woman trudging ahead of him. She tossed him an airy wave, dismissing him.

He looked down at her smaller footprints, fitting his boot beside them. He shouldn't have let her tear into him, rip open his heart and take the truth as if it were her right. They couldn't have had a future. She was angry now, but later she'd understand the reality....

Her mouth had tasted like fire and roses and dreams.

Ahead of him, Miranda stumbled and fell, and when Gabriel reached for her, she swatted him away. "Don't you *dare* touch me."

The fury wrapped in her words shocked him, stayed his hand. "You're tired and cold and too full of pride."

She launched to her feet as if anger had shoved

through her again, giving her extra strength. Her face was pale and taut, but her eyes were brilliant, lashing at him. *"Leave me alone."*

Uncertain how to handle her in this mood, Gabriel put away the horse as Miranda marched up to the house. It had taken every bit of his strength not to pick her up and place her on the horse. He had seen his petite mother match his father's temper with one dark look, and now Gabriel knew the force of a woman's fury. He decided to give her time to cool down, then try logic again. He shook his head; at this point he wasn't certain about Miranda's surprising flash-fire temper, her ability to take strips off him.

He paused before entering the house, carefully wiping his boots on the heavy outdoor mat. From the look of Miranda, he didn't know what to expect. She'd always been so cool and reasonable, and now temper ruled her.

Maybe his own was simmering, too. *He'd made the right choice for her all those years ago.* She'd gone on to become successful. She'd gone on to a man she'd chosen, a life that she fit into smoothly. Her anger wasn't justified, he reasoned, turning the doorknob and stepping into the firelit room. Miranda usually hung her clothing by the door, her boots placed neatly, side by side. Instead, this time she'd left a trail behind her that led into the kitchen area. There, she was dressed in her thermal underwear, glaring at him as she slapped peanut butter and jelly on bread.

Gabriel carefully removed his heavy winter outerwear, trying not to notice how the thermal silk clung to Miranda's curved body. "I am not in a good mood," she said warningly.

"Neither am I." She'd been crying, the paths still streaked her face. How could he have hurt her so? "What good would it have done to come to you? To tell you what was in my heart? So I left you to move on, into your life away from me and Freedom."

She held up the peanut butter knife to demonstrate her point. "Yet another decision on the part of Gabriel Deerhorn."

"Could we talk about this when you are rested?" To do something, anything, Gabriel picked up her sketchbook, studying the Celtic symbols woven and unending in their design. Miranda's intelligence was like that, sturdy and intricate and restless. She'd weave through everything he'd said, find the pattern of his need for her and lock onto it. He didn't have long to wait for her response.

She swiped the knife through the jam and held it to emphasize a point. "That's one more. You've just decided that I'm not logical enough now to think straight. I'm doing plenty of thinking now and I'm not tired. I'm angry. Boy, you're racking up the decisions here, Mr. Deerhorn. I settled for less than I wanted and I wanted you. *I settled for less because life has to go on and I couldn't spend my life mooning over someone who didn't want me, who didn't care enough to discuss the decision he had made for my welfare.*"

She reached over his shoulder for the bag of chips on the refrigerator. The contact of her soft breast against his chest sucked the breath from Gabriel. Miranda tensed, watching him, her eyes wide.

"You want me now, don't you?" she asked unevenly, her hand lowering to his shoulder, her fingers digging in. That quick green glance down his body locked on the intimate, undeniable thrust against his clothing. Then her eyes were clear, meeting his with a challenge.

There was no denying the effect she could have on him. Held too long, the truth exploded from him in a harsh admission. "Yes. I want to hold you and know that you are safe. I want to feel the beat of your heart against mine. To make you mine. It is in me now to take you, to make you my woman."

"I see. But this is my decision, isn't it?" Her gaze drifted over his lips, studying them, and Gabriel's heart leaped. Her fingertip slid along his brows, lowered down his nose and traced the outline of his mouth. He couldn't breathe as she stood on tiptoe, placing her mouth against his, those dark green eyes watching him. The play, the shared kisses, eyes open, tested Gabriel's resolve not to touch her, to take advantage of her. The flick of her tongue against his lips startled him and he jerked back, wary of her. She wore the look of a woman desiring a man, that closed-in, soft and hunting look.

Uncertain of what she wanted, or what game she now played, Gabriel shivered lightly. "What do you want, Miranda?"

"You," she whispered simply, and lowered her hand to unbutton the top of her silk undershirt. "Now."

Gabriel tried not to look at her body, those soft flowing curves, the flesh revealed in the opening, the shape of her breasts so close, he could— His hand trembled as he touched her, finding the delicate wonder of her breast within his hand, cuddling it gently.

Her sigh was that of pleasure, and desire danced
into flame between them. Holding his eyes, Miranda
eased off her undershirt, leaving her in the lacy bra
that had tormented Gabriel. "I want to hold you, too.
To know that you are safe and close against me. To
feel you inside me."

The bold erotic statement jarred Gabriel. He
wanted her to know that he was uncertain of his control and of how careful he would be of her. "I have
not had a woman in a long time."

"I know. That's why you're so nervous around me,
isn't it? You speak very properly when you are trying
to conceal your emotions. You're afraid of me, in
your way. Afraid you'll hurt me. I'm well now, Gabriel, in more than one way. I'm not vulnerable. I'm
angry, yes. I haven't decided how to handle that yet
as anger isn't something I deal with on a regular basis.
But I do know that you're not running from this, from
me." She leaned close, her breasts against him, burning him. Her body rested against his, her hips nestled
closely. "Just once, for tonight, lose that control, Gabriel, and show me what you feel. *I need to feel.*"

Her open lips on his caused him to tremble, forcing
back his need to— Then his hands opened on her
hips, tugging her closer, and he knew he was lost.

Miranda closed her eyes when he swung her up
into his arms. Somehow she'd always known that Gabriel would let his instincts rule him when he wanted
a woman desperately—his woman, the only woman
for him. He would move swiftly, claiming her, for
that was his hunter's nature. His heart raged against

hers, heat pouring from him, his hands holding her close, his body corded with the strength of desire.

His bedroom was cold, and yet she knew that he would take her to his bed, not hers. He lowered her to her feet, his hand circling her throat, a firm possessive touch, not threatening as his mouth came down again, swooping to fuse to hers. "Change your mind," he whispered raggedly, his lips hard against hers, feverish and tasting of desire just as she wanted. But he had stripped away her bra, his hands cupping her breasts, smoothing her trembling body as if researching the woman he would claim for a lifetime. "Leave me."

"No, I've waited too long, a lifetime, and I can't wait longer." She would not let him draw back, finding his mouth, claiming it, feeding upon him. The incredible sense of coming home ruled her, that for a time, she would know who she was, what she was intended to be…. *Gabriel…Gabriel…*

With shaking fingers, she fumbled with the layers of his clothing, his shirt, undershirt and with an impatient hiss of breath, Gabriel shed his clothing, standing before her bold, aroused and so alive. Heat shimmered in the cool air as his hands slid beneath the elastic waistband of her long silk pants and briefs. His rough palms and strong fingers spread over her bottom, holding her tight against him as he nuzzled her throat and gently nipped her earlobe.

He moved quickly, strongly, tugging her closer, as she arched against him. Lowering her to the bed, Gabriel lay over her, watching her. Those black eyes flickered down their bodies, hers pale and soft, tangled with his. There was nothing but the sound of their hearts now as Gabriel found and nudged her intimately.

Taking care, he eased slowly within her warmth, the incredible filling like magic, making her whole for the first time in her life. He shook against her, the muscles of his arms standing out in relief. That angular face above her displayed emotions she'd wanted all of her life—fierce, tender, amazed. There was male arrogance there, too, as if nothing could keep him from her. A look questioned her as she moved in the slow rhythm he had set, a familiar controlled rhythm with a different meaning. She knew he leashed himself, perspiration gleaming on his harsh face. The muscles bunched at his throat and shoulders told her the price he paid for keeping her safe.

"I'm fine," she whispered, fingers digging into his shoulders as she drew the incredible pleasure deep inside her. "Make love to me, Gabriel."

Seven

A man's pride is fragile as the petals of my
roses. To understand that pride is to peel away
the petals and thorns, and to listen to his fears.
He makes choices by a different standard than
a woman's sturdy heart. But when a woman
makes a choice, she is not apt to give it up
lightly—if it really matters.

Anna Bennett's Journal

Miranda lay within the cove of Gabriel's big warm
body and listened to the wind howling in the predawn.
She was exhausted from the trek in the mountains to
find him, tired of plodding through his reasoning, and
still furious with the years they had lost. Her thoughts
churning, she lay very still, her hand over his as it
cupped her breast, his thumb smoothing a caress.

He had touched her with reverence and care both times they had made love. His lips had moved over her body slowly, as if placing her in his memory forever. Incredibly sweet and tender, he'd given her everything, shattering her.

His heart beat steadily against her back now, and his thoughts echoed in the bedroom's shadows. "Miranda?"

She wasn't ready for the night to pass, yet a slice of brittle, harsh dawn pierced the window's curtain and reality would soon follow. The empty years that had passed between them slid over her; she shivered in the uncertainty that given the same choice, Gabriel would do the same. *She wouldn't.* She wouldn't settle for half a life again. A fine anger brewed in her now, pricked by his arrogance then and now. *I want you. I always have,* he'd said.

All those years… Miranda shivered, chilled by the thought that she might never have known…

Out there in the snowy mountain wild, he'd lost his temper, anger flying at her, and turned toward himself. The lid containing his emotions had come off for the first time, revealing that he *needed,* he *wanted,* he *dreamed.* Gabriel had kept all that from her, hoarded it for himself.

"Miranda?" he murmured again, this time his lips against her throat.

"I'm leaving," she whispered unevenly and fought the tear sliding down her cheek. The morning after making love with Gabriel she was too emotional. She wanted to compile the facts, sort through his admission that he'd always wanted her. "I need to think."

"I see." He tensed, but he didn't ask her why, or

to stay, and didn't say that he wanted her in his life. His quiet acceptance of what must be tormented her. That he'd expected her to leave angered her, inflamed the knowledge of the wasted years between them.

An hour later, Miranda shifted the gears on Gabriel's Jeep, driving down the mountain. In the rearview mirror, she saw him standing on the road, legs braced against the wind, hair flying untamed in the morning sun. He'd offered to drive her to Anna's, but she couldn't have that, tears too close to the surface.

Once on the highway, she couldn't drive straight to her mother's empty house. She circled the town, and found the sturdy, comforting familiarity of it.

Gabriel hadn't asked her to stay. He'd withdrawn again, as if their beautiful lovemaking had never happened.

She glanced at the church's white steeple, as the street's cobblestones rhythmically jarred the Jeep. There was Eli's Bakery and he'd be baking the cookies Gabriel loved so much. She drove to the cemetery and visited the gravesites where her mother and father and child were buried. If it hadn't been for the tragedy, her baby would have been due any day.... The chinook that could last for days swept over the valley and she knew she'd come full circle.

Only she could change her life and take what she wanted.

Miranda looked up to the mountains and knew that she wanted the man there.

Was she hurt by him? Yes. Miranda slid into Gabriel's Jeep and knew she was too tired to battle today. But if Gabriel thought he could make all the decisions in *her* life, he was mistaken.

*   *   *

Gabriel rubbed the ache in his chest and glanced at the garden seedlings beginning to sprout in Miranda's window boxes. It was only a few hours since she'd left him and it seemed like a cold eternity. It was for the best, he told himself repeatedly. He shouldn't have let her see into his heart, shouldn't have let her know that she'd haunted him all these years.

He shouldn't have made love to her. That memory could never be buried or washed away. He'd never forget the way she sighed luxuriously as he tasted her body, the way she moved so easily into his touch, opening to him, giving to him. He'd been careful, mindful of that slender, vulnerable, silken body.

She was angry with him now, for keeping his secrets. Given time, she would come to know that when they'd made love he'd been greedy for life, for her. But that their lives couldn't blend—he picked up the intricate Celtic symbols she'd drawn while coming back to herself. Interwoven, they were without end. He drew a fingertip across one design, severing the image of his and Miranda's lives intertwined. Gabriel shook his head. How could he sever the memory of their passion? How could he not remember the sweet yielding of her body, the softness of her sighs?

Gabriel drifted the palm of his hand across the dainty seedlings for a garden Miranda wished to make. For once the mountains did not call to him, the winds still howling her name, and having tasted the woman and the dream, he had never been so empty.

In the new pink dawn, he placed the tomato seedlings on Anna's step, wanting Miranda to have what she had sowed. The beaded moccasins were products of his hours, trying to stay away from her in his house, giving her time to think and heal.

On the window above the porch, Miranda watched Gabriel's tall body stride through the dawn, moving quickly away from her and what they could have had, could have now. Anger quivered within her now, but also excitement. For she had sowed more than seeds at Gabriel's house… His lovemaking mixed hunger with reverence, tenderness with passion, longing with fulfillment. There was no way she could turn away from that honest, frightening beauty—the insight Gabriel had given her with each touch, each breath. She'd glimpsed more in those few hours than she had in a lifetime and she would grasp it with both fists. She wanted a resolve between them—an equal resolve. "Like it or not, Mr. Gabriel Deerhorn, we are not finished yet. This time, I'm going to be included in the decision-making, whatever it may be."

Gabriel ladled water from the bucket onto the hot rocks of his sweat house. Midmorning seemed to hover in the first week of March, tiny slices of day penetrating the cracks between the small building's overhead boards; outside, blinding sunlight bounced off snow. When the snow melted, the nearby stream would become a small river tumbling down the mountain, feeding Valentina Lake. The weathered gray building, a distance from his house, was scented of the sage and sweet grass he had crumbled onto the coals. Steam slid through the pine boughs placed over the hot rocks and layered the small enclosure. On a plain wooden bench, Gabriel lay naked, sweat pour-

ing from his body, his hands folded behind his head.
He inhaled the purifying scents, gave himself to them,
and still could not rid himself of the need for Miranda.
Miranda.

She'd been so small and pale, lying in the snow at
the foot of her mother's steps. He'd never been so
terrified. She'd seemed empty later, too fragile,
mourning her child and her mother. Miranda seemed
as if her soul would pass through her skin at any
moment, escaping her keep.

The agony in her eyes as she saw her sister-in-law's
rounding body had been too much for Gabriel. His
need to protect Miranda, to keep her from harm, to
give her shelter, had been overwhelming.

Perhaps it was his father's blood that told him to
claim his woman, to keep her near.

Perhaps his needs were selfish, not only for Miranda's sake, but for the peace she brought him. Perhaps he took advantage of her—just to scrape that
small bit of time from the world and treasure it close
against him.

Two mornings ago Gabriel had wakened with her
in his arms. Was that a dream, the soft fragrance of
her haunting him? In her, he'd seen his eternity and
his essence, in that flashing pinpoint before his desire
came flooding into her keeping. He'd known that he
was meant to hold her, to give her his child, to keep
her safe until the winds took away their breath—together. She'd burned a path to his heart, and that soft
scar hurt him more deeply than those of the flesh.

Flesh? She was more—a part of him now, inside
him, moving in his blood, heating it, the fever for
her— Gabriel hadn't been aware of the power of a

woman's calling to him, and he wasn't certain about
his strength against it now—now that he had tasted
Miranda. He was angry with himself, and with her.
She'd torn away the pretense and exposed his need,
his dream of the woman in the smoke.

Bitterness curled from the scented steam into him.
He'd reached and taken. He'd tossed away reality and
devoured the few hours with her, reveled in them.
Perhaps when the winter years came to him, he would
know that it was a dream, and that he did not have
the right to touch her. Miranda was probably safely
on her way now…away from him.

Gabriel rubbed his hands over his damp face. *What
had he been thinking?*

Outside, Fletcher barked happily, probably chasing
a rabbit. Gabriel frowned; his house was no longer
barren, but softened by her woman's touch. The bedroom she had used, carried her fragrance.

*He would not expose himself to her again. He
would retain what little pride he had left.*

Gabriel reached for the ladle and just as he was to
pour it on the hot stones, the door of the sweat house
jerked open. A shaft of blinding midmorning sunlight
hit him, outlining a woman's long legs and curved
body.

The steam shifted, and catching the sudden sweeping blast of fresh air, the coals ignited, tiny flames
dancing around the pine needles. Then the door
closed and Miranda eased onto another bench, lying
down on it, her hands behind her head.

The slice of sunshine passing through the boards
on the roof softened as it fell on her long, curved
body, the dips and curves and fullness that marked

her as a woman. Scraps of lace covered her breasts and hips.

Perhaps he was dreaming; Gabriel lifted the ladle and poured the water over his head. He tried to remain calm, to cover his emotions while his heart leaped at the sight of her. "I suppose you think this is funny."

She turned slowly to him. In the half-light, her green eyes burned through the layers of steam to him, her face pale amid that shifting silky black hair. "I saw no reason to disturb your meditation. Please go ahead."

"You've come for your things. I will bring them back for you." He hadn't been able to stand the thought of wrenching her presence away from him.

"Don't you dare.... You talk too much."

Gabriel inhaled, the gentle verbal slap unfamiliar to him. He had always been a quiet man. He had— the steam had dampened the lace covering her, clinging to her, and Gabriel tried to remember what he had been about to say.

Miranda closed her eyes and placed her arms at her side, lying still, breathing slowly. Gabriel tried not to trace that long, soft body, the flow of her breast, the dip of her stomach, the jut of her hipbones and the slender strength of her thighs. He remembered the clamping pressure of them along his hips, the ebb and flow of her body against his, the cries that seemed drawn from her soul—

Gabriel rubbed his head and sat up. He poured water onto the rocks and fought his dancing nerves as the steam hissed. He rummaged for a logical protest and managed, "This is a man's place," he managed finally, firmly, in his best eviction notice.

She squirmed slightly on the wooden bench. The movement was sensuous, feminine and caused Gabriel's throat to tighten. She smiled slightly, drowsily as if settling into the steam and comfort. "Mmm. I know. It feels like you."

She was too quiet and Gabriel resented the question erupting harshly from him. "Why are you here?"

Miranda took her time in answering. "To set the terms."

Again, he was forced to pursue her. His mind cautioned, but he could not resist. "Terms?"

She stirred luxuriously, a strand of black hair clinging damply to her smooth cheek. "I have my pride. You have yours. Mine is no less than yours, Gabriel. It's time you recognized that."

"Pride does not come into this."

"So says you."

Gabriel frowned at the challenge, so unlike sweet teenage Miranda. She had crossed into a woman and he realized from experience with his mother and sister that feminine emotions were as safe as a lake's thin ice, or a wildfire searing the tops of the pines. Her gaze slowly took in his body as he sat, frowning at her. That dancing of his senses told him he wanted her, here and now. That primitive beat pounded him relentlessly.

"There's nothing here now but you and me," she said softly. "There is nothing else to consider. There is no past and no one else involved. Just you and me," she repeated.

"You know this isn't right." Gabriel scrubbed his shaking hands over his face. In another minute, he'd be moving over her, in her, that dark fever escaping his tethers— And where would it lead? Nowhere. Nothing had changed. Miranda was meant for one world, and his path was set for another, just as it was years ago. "What do you want?" he repeated darkly.

"I want the courting time we missed."

Gabriel shook his head and droplets of water sprayed across the layers of steam. Miranda's eyes were narrowed now, pinning him. "I have my pride, too. You took me in, gave me shelter at a time when I needed it. But I'm past that now, Gabriel, and you're going to have to deal with what has happened—will happen—between us. You can't shove me away. You cannot make my decisions for me. If you didn't want me, that would be one thing. But you do. It's in every look and touch—now that I see exactly how much you've withheld from me."

His answer was blunt and from the truth he knew. "It won't work."

"Well, for appearances at least, it's going to work for a while. I've already explained to Fidelity Moore and the ladies that I am handling you gently. In Freedom, you've apparently set an image for yourself as a confirmed bachelor. I simply explained that I wanted to give you more time to adjust to life with me, and that for a time, I wanted to court you, living at my house at times, easing you into a situation—"

"Dammit, I'm not to be trained. *And I am not delicate.*"

Miranda's summation of him was concise and slashed with anger. "No, you're just arrogant, hardheaded and need bringing down a notch. You think you can set terms? You think you can just waltz up to my home at dawn and give me the most beautiful, thoughtful, most romantic gift I've ever had, and then not take the consequences? You think you can come for me in that lovely old-fashioned way that meant so much to you—then discard me?"

"I did not discard you." Gabriel did not like the picture she presented. Freedom Valley had known he'd given the bridal price for her, that he'd come for her in the traditional way of his father's people. "The customs of Freedom Valley allow for a couple who try, but cannot weave their lives together."

"It's difficult to weave when you gave me nothing of yourself. Yes, you gave me a place to heal and the comfort of safety nearby. But you gave me nothing of what runs inside you, all that river of feeling that your eyes express and your body told me was the truth, not some cold excuse. You're afraid of me, Gabriel. You're afraid of intimacy with me, of giving me my due—that which is in your heart."

The challenge spread across the steam to him. Gabriel refused to answer her goad, to clash verbal swords with her.

Miranda sat up, frowning at him and Gabriel tried not to look at the dark, nubby circles outlined by the damp lace of her bra. He stared at the hot stones, which seemed more safe than Miranda just now. Still, he couldn't resist answering her taunt. He slapped the basic facts into the steamy enclosure. "How many degrees do you have, Miranda? How many do I have? What lifestyle suits you? What place? I can't see you living here with me, the hardships and—"

He glanced at her, that shaft of midmorning light cutting through the steam to capture Miranda's pale body, gleaming in the shadows. The need to take her, to claim her was too fierce, pounding at him. Taking a deep breath, Gabriel prepared to leave, and then Miranda's slender hand reached to flatten on his chest.

He trembled with desire, some inner instinct that told him to take her. Without force, that pale feminine hand over his heart tethered him. "I've come to court you, Gabriel," Miranda whispered softly. "Do you refuse me?"

Could he refuse the air coming into his body, sustaining him? Could he refuse the sun that heated the earth, the rain that nurtured it?

Could he refuse the woman he loved as she shed the damp lace and moved sleekly, damply, warmly into his arms?

Then the fever and the hunger that was Miranda took Gabriel Deerhorn, leaving him no defense, no logic. Their bodies slid together as if they were meant to be—

In his house, forty-five minutes later, Gabriel shook his head as Miranda emerged from her shower wearing only his chambray shirt. Folded turban-style, the white towel around her head emphasized her brilliant green eyes. She found him in the shadows of the kitchen area and her brisk efficient movements slowed, her gaze slumberous as it strolled over his bare chest and jeans. "Why, Gabriel. I do believe you're sulking," she murmured.

Gabriel was methodically making sandwiches and trying to assemble what had happened. With one touch, Miranda had destroyed his vow to separate his life from hers, freeing her. He was still stunned at how he'd taken her there in the sweat house, on the floor covered with toweling. This time had been different, for Miranda's fever fed his own, her teeth nipping at his shoulder, her fingers digging into his back. He rolled a shoulder, suspecting the marks she had left, the pleasure that had riveted him as she came into that trembling pulse of her release. Gabriel prowled through his thoughts carefully: he suspected that Miranda's passions could tear away his leashes, his intentions to be gentle with her. Just there, with her tossing beneath him, fever hot, their bodies sliding, he'd held her, possessed her, dived in to take what was his. A controlled man, Gabriel had held her hips and lifted them— He closed his eyes, the primitive scene locked in his mind. And as he held her, she held him, a match for the fiery need. He shouldn't have handled her so roughly—cupping her hips, finding her breasts with his lips, tasting her...

His hand trembled as he sliced tomatoes for the bacon sandwiches. "I have the feeling you just counted coup—won a small victory and scored a point for your side."

"I love feeling like a woman. You make me *feel*, Gabriel."

He studied this woman who could seem so delicate and yet he recognized her inner and physical strength—she could be both fierce and sweet when making love.

Miranda stood on tiptoe to brush her lips against one corner of his lips and then the other. Gabriel held onto the counter to keep from floating as she slanted him a look and placed a strip of bacon into his mouth. "I drove your Jeep up here with one of your horses tied behind it. I'll be riding the horse back down."

Gabriel tensed, the image of the big cougar he'd seen slashing through his mind. "No, you're not."

"I'm staying in Freedom Valley, Gabriel. I'm not running away and I won't be pushed away. You're going to have to deal with me." Those clear meadow-green eyes searched his face. She skipped from the argument he was prepared to meet into another dazzling realm. "You either lock me out in defense, or run. And I want all of you. I don't want you to protect me, to think of my best interests, to feed me, or anything else, unless it's a policy that can be returned in kind. See that you let me carry my share now, will you? Are you going to let me court you?"

Miranda placed her forehead against his shoulder in the old, trusting way and Gabriel fought yielding to the sweet enticement. "It's a silly thing," he said finally, his senses reeling with the fresh scent of her. "A woman should not court a man."

Then Miranda lifted her mouth to his and the searing hunger drove all else away. Each time he touched her, the need rose more quickly. He couldn't resist looking down at the soft body resting against him, and unbuttoned her shirt. Her breasts came into his hands as if they belonged in his keeping. The taste of them curled on his tongue, demanding more.

His hands swept down the indentation of her waist and opened to lock onto her hips, the veed shadows of her womanhood beckoning to him. He thought of the woman in the smoke: Miranda softly curved with his child and he pushed the treasured dream away. She trembled, and worried that his obvious need frightened her, he scanned her expression. Miranda's smooth hands framed his face, her thumbs soothing the corners of his mouth. Her eyes were clear and green as summer grass. "Love me exactly how you feel," she whispered. "No pretenses, no logic, no fear of hurting me. In this, give me honesty, what your senses tell you is right."

He closed his eyes and her flowing Celtic symbols came to him, the strength and the curve and the endless need that had increased with each touch.

Later, he drove her to her home, met the softness of her lips, and then alone again in his barn, wondered what he had done. He rubbed the ache in his chest, and shook his head. Miranda's courting of him chafed, the roles reversed. Freedom Valley was based on women taking the lead in dating customs and that put him at Miranda's disposal. He wasn't certain if he liked that or not. It was only a temporary game, he decided, Miranda's mind and body coming alive... nothing could come of it and then she'd be gone. *Miranda....* "Maybe I am delicate," he admitted and wondered what her next move would be.

Gabriel blinked, the thought pinning him very still, wrapping around him. *He was the hunted. She made the rules.* "This is very unwise," he said to the airy barn and didn't like the uneven sound of his voice.

Eight

When Miranda's turn comes to court a man, she
won't be wanting the easiest of the pack. She'll
want one with all the little edges to explore and
tame. Despite her orderly and ladylike appearance, she can be quite the hunter and needs a
match to her game.

Anna Bennett's Journal

"**S**top scowling," Miranda murmured easily. She
glanced at Gabriel, seated next to her in her new red
pickup. "You look like you're being hauled into
Doomsday."

Gabriel sat with his arms crossed. The pickup was
small; his knees bent sharply to accommodate the
length of his legs. It was better than revealing his fear
of Miranda's driving by holding on to the dashboard.

The next bump on the road leading from his house took his head against the roof and jarred his knees lightly against the dashboard. He refused to rub the slight injury. "I could have driven down the hill to your mother's house."

He hadn't liked waiting for her to drive to collect him—"collect him," as if he were a helpless... The reversal of roles called for by Freedom Valley's courting system chafed him once again. In waiting for Miranda, he had changed clothes several times and nothing seemed right. He was a hunter, bred to stalk his prey, collecting it, and now as a potential groom candidate, he was very vulnerable and uncertain. No matter what his feelings were, how contrary being placed on an inspection block, he wouldn't let Miranda down. At the last minute, he'd made a silly trip down the mountain, hurrying to purchase new jeans and a light blue dress shirt. He'd shined his best boots and belt and buckle. Miranda's party was important to her, and Gabriel sensed that amid Miranda's family and friends, he would be inspected as a suitable match for her. *He wasn't.*

By using the old system of messages by homing pigeons, he thought darkly, he was safe, not aroused by the tone of her husky voice. Why then had he ordered a new telephone line? This uncertain fragile-male business did not sit well with Gabriel Deerhorn.

Gabriel inhaled and braced for the next rut, which she hit as surely as if she'd been aiming for it. She glanced at him. "Stop shaking your head. You'll live."

"I've got magazine photographers coming up to-morrow. They're staying for a week and I'm guiding them in the high country. A concussion would make that difficult." He resented his bad mood and grumping. His life was no longer smooth and comfortable. The next bump jarred her breasts, which quivered beneath a soft green material concealed by her long coat. Her scent wafted to him, erotic, enticing....

She patted his knee. "I'll be careful with you, baby. I'll get you home in plenty of time to rest up. About that guide trip. I don't suppose you'd invite me along?"

"It's all men." *Baby.* She was teasing him, and Gabriel refused to take the bait.

"What does that have to do with anything?"

He felt like a stag protecting his harem of one precious woman from intruders. How could he explain that logically, even to himself? "We're camping.... Bathroom facilities," he muttered and his mind swung to another danger—Freedom Valley's Bachelor Club. "Has Brody come around? Koby? Fletcher?"

"Uh-huh, all of them. They're going to be at my party tonight. I think Mom would have liked all of us together in her house. I enjoyed the preparations— good food, Mom's punch recipe, baking bread and cakes... And I'm not buying that 'bathroom facilities' logic."

Gabriel settled into his dark thoughts of the potential poachers surrounding his woman. "But your hope chest is still at my house," he said, carefully reaffirming his temporary rights to Miranda.

"Yes, it is." She glanced at him. "You look very nice, Gabriel."

"Thank you." The words were tightly begrudged and dark and unlike him.

Anna's house was already lit up, cars and trucks parked carefully so as not to disturb her yard. Gabriel braced himself as he followed Miranda into the house, filled with laughter and chatter and good friends. At the back door, she replaced her serviceable winter boots with his beaded moccasins, and a bit of his uncertainty dissolved. Gabriel tried to shake off his image as a territorial male, and failed the first time Miranda stood on tiptoe to hug and kiss each of her guests—which included all of Freedom Valley's known women-hunting bachelors.

With large gold hoop earrings and a matching emerald tunic and flowing slacks, she moved easily through the role of hostess. Little remained of the pale, hurt woman who had first come to his home. She didn't need him now, he thought whimsically. Miranda had always been very capable, very organized, and now amid her friends and family, she laughed easily. Her green eyes danced with a tidbit Tanner had remembered of their childhood, a time when Miranda and Kylie had surprised him and his friends while they were skinny-dipping.

"Don't even think about it," Gabriel ordered lightly to Dakota Jones, who was woman-chasing for a mother for those children he wanted.

"You're going to have to step out more often, old man," Dakota returned easily with a grin. "Miranda likes this—family and friends around her. Look at how she glows. She's all lit up and you sure as hell can't be the reason. You haven't said much all night, and everyone knows you prefer your mountains to a crowd like this.''

Koby Austin, who had lost a wife and son to childbirth, sipped Anna's aged blackberry wine and studied Miranda, then Gabriel. ''Too bad about her baby—your baby.''

Dylan Spotted Horse nodded. ''A real shame. If I'd been the one she wanted, I wouldn't have kept it a secret, visiting her away from Freedom Valley.''

Brody Thor, who had married at seventeen and had raised his daughters alone after his wife deserted them, nudged Gabriel with his shoulder. ''I have a hard time believing that story, because I know you. If that baby were yours, she would have been wearing your ring. You're an old-fashioned man, Gabriel. You'd have lassoed her into marriage right away.''

Gabriel closed into himself, shielding his thoughts. Apparently his friends knew about the lie told to protect Miranda. In all possibility, any one of them would have done the same. He tried to concentrate on Dakota's sister, Karolina, as she asked him questions about the old outlaw's grave, reputed to be in the high country he roamed. But he worried about Miranda, the way she placed her hand on Gwyneth's round body, feeling the child nestled within. The delight in Miranda's expression said that her own trial had slid somewhat into the past. She laughed outright as she placed her other hand on Kylie's as yet flat stomach.

Gabriel's heart stopped as she turned, green eyes sparkling. She found him in the crowded room and the rising flush on her cheeks told him that she recognized him as her lover. The moment danced between them, softly, sweetly, laced with a mixture of sensuality and tenderness and memories of a wildflower bouquet between them and that first heavenly, sweet kiss. She moved toward him, and he went dizzy just looking at her. The conversation became a buzz, the people he'd known for a lifetime fading into the background. Then Miranda stood in front of him, her expression one of pleasure.

There was little he could do but lower his lips to her soft ones.

Five days later, Gabriel ignored the men grousing about the freezing mid-March wind on a high, rocky mountain peak—perfect for photographs of the bighorn sheep nearby. He settled into the warmth of Miranda's lovemaking, the taste of blackberry wine and happiness on her lips, and knew that he was no longer complete without her. His mind told him that she would soon leave, taking his heart with her. He braced himself for the lonely life ahead and for a time gave himself to the cleansing wind and the stars above, allowing his soul to flow to hers, twining together like the campfire smoke. He felt her in his body, pulsing, the warmth of her embracing him, those grass-green eyes drowsy in the aftermath of lovemaking. His hand curled within his heavy glove, sensitive to a softer texture, her flesh cruising along his body, drifting in his mind.

He'd invited her into his home after her party and once inside, he'd tugged her to him, hungry for her, the fire raging between them instantly. That primitive need to claim her could not be restrained.

His body sprung to her touch too easily, leaving

him little resistance. Each time she came to him, she left him less complete than before.

She would leave soon enough, that brilliant mind needing challenges Freedom Valley could not offer....

Gabriel opened his eyes to the night, the men huddling around the campfire, cleaning their expensive camera gear. She belonged to their world, business-savvy, smart, brain crunching numbers, logic layering every thought. What did he have to offer Miranda?

With his teeth, Gabriel tore away a chunk of dried deer jerky and chewed it without tasting. He'd been right the first time—to set her free, and after a long week away from the sensual needs of their bodies, Miranda's laser-sharp mind would be defining reality. She would define her life apart from his, recognize the folly of any relationship between them.

Gabriel scanned the night, listened to the wind in the trees and the animals that were a part of him. She could never be a part of his world, and his spirit, the strength of his essence, could never live in hers....

The savage, deep bloodred pulsing fever her scent could cause in him, or even one look from those dark green eyes—the need to mate with her, to give her his child, made him uneasy. Now it lurked inside him, humming when he would have peace.

Fletcher was restless, pacing the camp with raised hackles, a sign of a dangerous animal nearby. A man lit a cigarette, killing it when Gabriel stared coolly at him. The "man" smell, carried by the wind, would drive away any animals.

Or attract the big cat stalking them.

The next afternoon, Gabriel's binoculars pinned the bright red jacket, the slight figure of Miranda, bent against the forceful wind. On a rocky ledge above her, the cougar was sunning and watching her. Suddenly the cat was on his feet, his body crouched to stalk.

Gabriel quickly told the men to stay put, to watch for the cougar, and that he would return. At a run, with Fletcher at his side and his rifle slung to his back, Gabriel plunged into the thick pines, fear icing his blood, pushing him to his limits. *Miranda...*

Terrorized that he would cause the cougar to react, harming Miranda, Gabriel closed the distance, motioning for Fletcher to be silent. They hunted together now, man and dog, trained to notice and interpret the slightest movement of the other.

In the clearing, Miranda stood poised, a rifle to her shoulder. Wind whipped at her blue-black gleaming hair, released from the coat's hood. On a rocky ledge above her, the cougar was poised to leap. Gabriel forced himself not to yell, and moved silently closer. He could miss the long shot, only wounding the cougar and Miranda would be in more danger. To distract the cougar, focused now on Miranda, was safer. He heard the noises of the approaching men behind him and damned them for the complication that could cost Miranda's life. Without distracting Miranda, Gabriel inched closer, and motioned for Fletcher to circle the cougar.

"Miranda," Gabriel said quietly and moved forward, rifle in hand, placing himself between her and the snarling, crouched cougar.

Her voice was an uneven thread, caught on the wind. "Gabriel. Don't—"

Everything happened at once: Fletcher barked, startling the cougar. It leaped on Gabriel, who was closer, and Miranda fired. Torn from him by the feline's impact, his rifle was useless. Battling the wiry, strong mountain lion, Gabriel protected his throat and the slash of claws burned his thigh.

He rolled with the cougar and heard a second shot; pain stabbed into his left buttock and the cougar slumped upon him.

Pinned beneath the wildcat and stunned, his thigh burning, Gabriel distantly heard the sound of clicking cameras, saw their glass eyes focus at him as Fletcher barked excitedly in the distance. Heart pounding, Gabriel pushed off the limp beast, struggled to his feet and caught Miranda, who flew into his arms. He tugged back her hair, read the stark fear in her face, the tears streaming down her cheeks. *She was safe.*

He dived into her kiss, locked onto it and forgot everything but the joy in knowing she was alive and unharmed. She tore herself from him, then bent to see his leg, the torn cloth soaked with blood. "We've got to get him to medical help. I need a tourniquet.... Now!"

Gabriel's icy fear still held him. He didn't know if it was Miranda shaking, or his heart, trying to leap free of his body. He wrapped a fist in her collar and tugged her upright in front of him. His fear shifted into anger. "You could have been killed. What are you doing up here?"

She dashed away her tears with her glove, her eyes fierce and green and lashing at him. "Tracking that cat. His prints are all over your yard. Then I saw them heading in the same direction as your regular trail— it was muddy and the prints were clear—and I couldn't bear to have him hurt your less than affectionate hide. You had no business placing yourself between him and me. If you had only stayed out of this, you wouldn't have gotten hurt. Now see what you've done.''

Now see what you've done.... The words seemed to echo in the distance and Gabriel shook his head to clear the weak, drowsy feeling. Perhaps it was his reaction to the shock of seeing Miranda facing the cat. Perhaps it was the toll of fear—

''I'm sorry I shot you in the butt with that tranquilizer, dear heart,'' Miranda was saying somewhere near him as his head went floating off into the wind and his body sagged heavily into the men's arms. She bent low to him and tugged the stinging dart from his backside. ''I was aiming for the cougar. We'd better get out of here, guys, before that cat comes awake. It's a pretty light dose, that's why I thought a second one might be okay. Please be careful with Gabriel.''

''We've been with this guy for five days and four nights, lady. He's made out of leather,'' one of the photographers said in the distance. Gabriel tried to make his mouth move, but his lips were thick and useless, his tongue not obeying his command.

''Shush. He could hear you. You'll hurt his feelings. He's very sensitive about some things. Come on, let's move. We'll use my sleeping bag to fashion a stretcher for him,'' Miranda crooned from another galaxy. Her voice came harder then, more determined as Gabriel struggled against the heavy weight in his brain and body. ''An emergency medical kit? Great. Whiskey? Great, the alcohol will disinfect the wound. Make that stretcher—cut holes in the bottom of the

bag and put those two branches through the bag. Give
me a knife, someone. I'll disinfect and wrap this.''

Cold liquid poured over his leg and pain seared
through him, bringing Gabriel close to the surface,
and he struggled to defend his pride and honor. ''I
am not 'less than affectionate.'''

The men's laughter angered him, but there was little he could do as he drifted off again. He was barely
aware of the trek down the mountain, and then Dr.
Thomas White, a frequent visitor to Freedom Valley,
was bending over him. Dressed in slacks and a matching vest, Thomas's immaculate dress shirt was folded
back at the cuffs. ''I was just passing through on the
road to Freedom when the call came in from Ella, the
sheriff. Seems like one of your photographer guests
has more sense than you do and packs a mobile telephone. I was here when they packed you in like a big
game trophy. Seems like you had a nice sleep down
the mountain, except for rousing enough to spout
some pretty romantic stuff—something about the
grass-green of her eyes, the petals of her lips—''

When Thomas caught Gabriel's scowl, he paused,
grinned and then continued. ''She's done a fine job,
keeping you off that leg. The wound isn't bad and
you've got a few minor scratches. You lost some
blood and the exertion as you fought with the cougar—when combined with the tranquilizer—caused
you to go night-night pretty quickly. Offhand, I'd say
you'd been missing some sleep—probably working
on those neat little romantic phrases, like 'the sunlight
of my heart' and 'wild rose beauty.' You've got a
few stitches and probably a scar or two—good brag-

ging material for those children you'll probably have one day."

"He's angry and pouting," Miranda said quietly. "He didn't want me to help him."

Thomas chuckled. "He's the old-fashioned type. He's brooding because you've stolen his thunder. He wanted to protect you and I would say that he did his job. That cat could have hurt you badly before falling asleep. Gabriel had the strength to hold it off, until the tranquilizer did its job."

Lying in his bed, Gabriel ignored Thomas, and found Miranda in the shadows. He had stoically managed to let her sponge his face and neck, because the unique sensation of her fretting over him, tending him with such care, was too enticing to resist. His adamant protest had died the moment she placed her hand on his forehead. "You endangered yourself. You could have been killed."

"Mr. Deerhorn thinks he's the only person who can lend a helping hand. He resents his current position of being the person who needs help. I chose to go up that mountain. I was safe enough until you entered the ball game. I read the directions for the tranquilizers that you keep on hand. I am sorry to have shot you, though."

"She's a highly intelligent woman, who can make do under the worst of circumstances. She stayed behind to tranquilize the cougar again when it started to come to—giving the men more time to get you to safety…. If you hadn't been wrestling with that cougar, she wouldn't have shot you in the butt, old man," Thomas murmured, his narrow, aristocratic face alight with pleasure.

The men's voices outside Gabriel's bedroom echoed in what seemed to be a toast. ''Here's to Old Shot
in the Butt!''

''I know where she hit me,'' Gabriel returned too
sharply and resented his frustration as he slid once
more into sleep.

When he awoke, it was to the sound of his tractor
revving up the morning. The smell of coffee filled the
house, his leg throbbed, and after his sponge bath, the
bandage didn't fit well inside his jeans. Managing to
dress in jeans and a flannel shirt, Gabriel limped to
the kitchen and resented his weakness. Morning sunlight slashed through the windows as he poured the
coffee, sipping it. At least the men were gone now,
their taunting cheer still hovering in the silence of his
home.

On the countertop was a stack of large glossy
black-and-white photographs from one of the men. A
note explained that he had developed them in the
kitchen sink with a very adept student, Miranda. Several photographers had added their notes, thanking
him for the best action shots they'd had in their careers. Bracing himself, Gabriel studied the photographs, one by one—just there, Miranda, looking
small and helpless against the highland meadow, dotted with snow, the cougar poised on the rock above
her. In black-and-white, Gabriel and Fletcher blended
with the trees. Gabriel's profile was hard, a hunter
determined to bring down his prey. Miranda's face
was white with fear, her eyes rounded as he moved
in front of her. The cat's fangs were bared, muscles
standing out in relief. One photograph was of the
beast flying in midair with Gabriel beneath its

shadow. The nightmare of the attack had been caught, and then the still body of the cat.

He'd held Miranda so close—he could feel the shaking of her body still, the fear leaping around them. One photograph held his attention—Gabriel had tugged Miranda's head back. The mountain wind had caught his shaggy hair, her sleek silky mass, and tossed them together, framing her fierce defiance, his primitive emotions in stark black-and-white.

Gabriel pushed away the close-up of the dart in his backside and frowned at the pictures of Miranda working over him, the men loading him onto the makeshift stretcher. Outside his house, the tractor revved and Gabriel limped to the doorway. The sun told him it was midmorning, the long furrows in his front door told him that the cougar had come calling.

Miranda swung the tractor and set the plow's tines into the rich earth. Breaking ground for the new garden gave her something to do while Gabriel rested up for another round of arguing with her. Within her gloves, her hands were shaking on the controls of Gabriel's tractor. He was limping toward her, and just as she had expected, his expression was that of lightning and thunder.

He'd been so pale, the blood gushing from the long scores on his thigh, soaking his jeans. The image of the man and the beast rolling on the mud and the snow would terrify her forever.

In the bright sunlight, Gabriel's hackles were up, a scowl etched on his darkly tanned face. Clearly he was set on an argument. Well, so was she. She'd lain beside him, soothed him as he tossed in his nightmares and tried to place the quaking fear into the past. His wounds could have been much more serious, but perhaps Gabriel was part leather—at least he was strong and had protected himself as best he could. *He'd placed himself between her and danger without a qualm....*

This morning, his expression said she was in for a scolding. Gabriel's emotions were usually so tightly leashed that she wanted to tear them away into the fresh spring air, revealing the deep natural emotions of the man. Tranquilized, he had murmured the most romantic phrases she'd ever heard, and they were all for her. He spoke of his heart leaping like a rabbit at the sight of her, how her skin was pale as cream, her scent of wild roses, that she was his woman of wind and fire— *How dare he hoard all that from her?*

She turned off the tractor, leaped from it and marched across the plowed ground toward him. She whipped off the red bandanna covering her hair. "Feeling better?" she asked briskly.

Gabriel scowled down at her, erasing the image of the romantic, tranquilized man holding her hand, kissing it. Once she had bent close to hear him whisper how he felt in her arms, filling her, feeling her glove him, his body pouring into hers, the fire of his passion for her....

Now Gabriel's tone ripped across the crisp March morning. No 'sweetheart,' no 'wild rose of my heart,' no 'thank you very much' or 'I love you.' "When was that cat here?" he asked harshly.

Her temper simmering, Miranda could have flung herself at him. "Before it took off the mountain after you. You're going after it, aren't you?"

"Someone has to. The wildlife people will probably mark and transport it elsewhere."

"Just like you'd like to do with me, right?" *Oh, Gabriel. Take me in your arms like you did then, let me know how much you care and that you want me so fiercely that nothing can take me away....*

"I don't want you working my place."

"I'm plowing a garden, not logging. Though at this moment, I'm so angry with you that I could take down a forest and not even be winded."

"A man should take care of his woman." His deep, soft voice was ragged, though he looked off into the pasture where the horses were grazing.

"Cannot a woman take care of her man, Gabriel?" she asked softly.

His cold black gaze swung down to her. "You don't belong here. This incident just proves me right. You could have been killed."

She shrugged and nodded. "Mark another one of my choices up to your side."

"Be logical. You're a remarkable woman. You belong—"

She walked toward the house, leaving him standing in the field. She had her pride, too, and she wouldn't ask him to reconsider. She wouldn't argue. She wouldn't—

Gabriel caught the door she tried to slam behind her, just a brief release for the frustration, anger and emotions storming her. She wrapped her arms around her body, unable to move, to leave him, when so much of her wanted to hold him, to love him, to hear those dark lush whispers of his passion.

His breath was harsh behind her, then he was tugging her back against him, wrapping his arms tight around her. His deep voice was uneven and urgent against her ear. "You think I don't want you? You, the other part of my heart and soul? When will you hate me, I wonder? When will you see that I can give you so little?"

"Is it only for *you* to give, Gabriel? Are you only comfortable in that one-way street where you are the provider and the protector? I'm a complete package now, Gabriel, and it is not in my nature to be helpless. If you can understand nature, and live with it, why can't you deal with who I am now?" *He gave her so much, that intricate, delicate part of him that no one had seen, the beauty of his soul, the gentleness of his heart.*

He spun her toward him, his expression fierce and desperate. He cupped her face within his roughly callused palms, scanning her expression. "You terrify me," he whispered simply before taking her mouth with undisguised passion.

She understood the need to celebrate life, to grasp it and revel in the survival of a past danger. She opened herself to him, taking from him, meeting that burning passion as his hand found her breast and cherished it softly. The fever rose between them and suddenly Gabriel stilled, the sound of tearing cloth echoing in the room. He shook, his hand trembling as he lifted it away from the flannel shirt she wore, the buttonholes torn free to reveal the dangling strap of her lacy bra.

Gabriel paled slightly, shaking his head as if to clear it, and Miranda wouldn't let him retreat. She reached for his cotton shirt and tore it open. "I want you just as badly now. Let me know what you really feel. Tell me with your body, if not with words.''

He hesitated, seemingly caught between the wars of his logic, his heart and his body. The burning fever of his hand touched her breast, then with a tug tore the remaining lace away. Holding her eyes, he eased her jacket away and bent to unlace her boots, removing them. His hands skimmed up her legs, her hips, unbuttoning her jeans to slide them away with her briefs.

Then Gabriel was carrying her to his bed, his mouth hot and sweet and hungry and urgent. He placed her onto his bed, the rumpled blankets carrying his scent. His trembling hands, the way he fumbled with his clothing, told her that he was deeply moved, anxious not to hurt her and yet driven by his own need for completion.

This was the real Gabriel, she thought, the layers gone, his eyes burning down the length of her body, consuming her, taking away her breath with that hunter's hungry look. He came to her quickly, his hands smoothing her body, finding her intimately, and caressing her.

The rough gauze reminded her of his painful wound and she pushed away from him, bracing her hands against his shoulders. That quick, dark expression told her too much, that he thought she refused him. Miranda wrapped her hands in his hair, drawing his head down, feasting upon his mouth to leave no doubt of her need. In the shadows, she briefly noted his honed features, the flush on his cheeks and the hardness of his body arched against hers.

Then his mouth was moving over her skin, nipping,

tasting, kissing. She cried out as he reached her breasts, suckling and giving her exquisite pleasure. "You're burning," he whispered roughly, cupping her, his fingers invading her delicately. "Soft and tight and so sweet."

She dug her fingers into the powerful muscles of his shoulders, her hips stirring restlessly against his touch, her legs moving along his. "Please be careful of your wound."

His tender smile curved along her stomach. "You would ask that of me now?" he chided gently. "When all of me is dying to fill you? When my skin is bursting with the need to become one with you? To feel your body move against me? To know that you soar with me into the fire? That the song of your release is too sweet to describe?"

"You're teasing me," she whispered shakily, uncertain of Gabriel's mood, when she had expected him to take her immediately.

"The honey of your skin is not a taste I can forget. I'm honored that you battle to give me such joy." His tongue flicked her naval, his hand spanning her belly. "Woman of fire and wind."

"Is that how you see me?" She quivered as his warm face pressed against her breasts, nuzzling them tenderly.

"Maybe." His answer came too lightly, tormenting her. He studied her breasts, tracing a finger enticingly over the sensitized surface, the jutting of her hardened nipples. With that, Gabriel eased to his back, his arms behind his head, and shot her a sultry, burning look beneath his lashes. "Be gentle," he whispered in a deep tone that curled around her.

She hadn't suspected that he would play, when his lovemaking had been so consuming, so serious and driving. She smiled and moved upon him. She closed her eyes and gave herself to the wonderful sensation of Gabriel's desire filling her, his hands opened and locked on her hips, caressing her. She rocked gently, bracing her hands on his chest, giving herself to the pleasure. "Oh, I intend to be very gentle and very thorough. Statistics prove that men like—''

"Concentrate on this man, song of my heart."

Nine

There is a part of any man which resists the woman selecting him as her mate, for he would like to think he has made that choice. The man's instincts are still to hunt and bring the woman to his lair—and so it is that we sometimes let them have their way.

Anna Bennett's Journal

Gabriel sat on his haunches, studying Anna's house in the night. He was bone-tired from tracking and tagging the cougar with the wildlife agent. The animal was now in a holding cage and would be relocated.

Gabriel's hunting blood was too restless to settle for the night, and Miranda was not in his house. What had he expected? She was a woman to make her own decisions.

She was still angry with him, for the years they had lost, for taking away her choice. He had felt the fine, prickling edge of her temper, though they had made love. She'd wanted to go with him, was nettled when he refused. But Gabriel couldn't bear the thought of her near that beast again.

What drove him to run on foot through the night, in the old way, hunting what his heart must have for peace? Though he had only run five miles, taking the paths that would bring him more quickly to Anna's house, he would have crossed much more to have her this night.

" 'Less than affectionate,' " he repeated, the phrase nipping at him. He glanced at the moon, pine trees spiking silhouettes across it. A fastidious man, he smelled of campfire smoke and leather and of battle. He should have stopped at his house, showered, rested and gotten his need for her under control. And yet, he couldn't wait to hold her. The wildfire in his blood was not in his experience, the need to capture the treasure that had escaped him.

Gabriel rubbed his jaw, considering the yellow squares of light shooting from Anna's windows onto the ground. The ache in his heart could not let him rest until he saw Miranda, despite the fatigue lodged in his muscles. Without turning from his view of Anna's house, he frowned at deer moving through the brush. He recognized their sounds, understood their ways, but not his own.

A woman's shadow moved across the upstairs windows and Gabriel wondered if she were packing, preparing to leave. He held very still, listening to the night and to the hard beat of his heart, focusing inside himself. Lying beside him, Fletcher panted, his pink tongue dangling, and waited for his master's command.

Fifteen minutes later, Gabriel frowned at the locked door separating him from his quarry. His knock unanswered, Gabriel circled the house, located a big tree and began to climb. Five minutes later, he shoved open an upstairs window and entered Miranda's bedroom. Moonlight shafted through the window's lacy curtains, laying patterns over the quilt on the single bed, the dolls' faces staring at him from their shelf. On the dresser were framed pictures, an array of feminine bottles and a braided rug cut from old clothing covered the wooden floor. The light rectangular place on the floor was where Miranda's hope chest had stood, and now it was in his home.

He noted the open laptop computer on a small wooden desk, small gold earrings gleaming beside it. Gabriel's senses stopped as he studied the electronic tool that she would use in her work. Did the challenges of her career call to that bright, quick mind? Was she feeling the need to step back into business? How soon would she leave?

How could he keep her? Did he deserve to have her now?

How could he keep her? his mind repeated, while his body knew that she was his tonight—if she would have him. *For he needed her like the air he breathed, like the sun that warmed the earth....* Already his blood was rushing into the fever that was Miranda.

Gabriel carefully removed his denim jacket and hung it on the desk's chair. The masculine clothing was at odds with the lace and ruffles, giving him the

same pleasure as when he looked at their coats, side
by side, her smaller boots placed neatly beside his.
Those were images he would carry in his mind forever, having no need of a camera to hold them. In his
mind, he was married, for he would never love another woman as he did Miranda. Pinned by a moonlit
square, slipping through the window's lace, Gabriel
considered his well-worn comfortable tracking moccasins. In his heart, he was coming home to the
woman of his soul, because she gave him strength
and peace. The sound of the shower drew him to the
bathroom, and Miranda's body, blurred by the frosted
glass, beckoned to him. Scented of her, the steamy
air curled around him. Gabriel stood very still, the
scent and the woman a seduction.

Caught in the mirror, his image was that of a
hunter—that narrowed look, features honed within the
rough cut of his long hair, body taut and prepared to
move. Gabriel glanced at the feminine lace hung on
the back of the door, crushed it in his fist, holding it
tightly for a moment as he would soon hold Miranda—if she would have him.

He should have called—he should have waited.

He smiled briefly, mocking himself. But then he
couldn't wait, could he? His need for her was too
strong.

Miranda inhaled sharply, the glass shower door
sliding open and a tall, naked man dipped his head to
enter. ''Gabriel!''

In the small steamy enclosure, he looked so drained
and weary, lines deeper on his brow, his hair untamed
and damp now against his throat. He needed care and
rest, she thought, and noted with pleasure as she

glanced lower, that Gabriel needed more— He filled
the space, towering over her, and then shook his head
as if dazed at finding himself with her.

"Have a nice hunt?" she asked lightly, as though
he were just coming home from a day's work at the
office, not the dangerous trek to hunt the cougar. He
was uncertain of her now, and of himself.

He was safe. She could have leaped upon him,
taken him, burned with him and yet, Miranda wanted
to savor the moment—for he had come to her, placing
all else aside. She squirted herbal shampoo into her
palms, rubbed them together and lifted her hands to
massage Gabriel's hair. He lifted his head, his expression disdaining the feminine scent and then he
settled into her touch. His eyes closed slightly, and
she sensed the easing of that taut, wary mood riding
him.

Miranda smoothed his face and he sighed slowly,
relaxing slightly. How wonderful, she thought, as this
tall, powerful man gave himself to her touch. Using
her sponge laden with shower gel, she slathered his
shoulders, admiring the strength in them, the gentleness that came of his consideration and control. His
heart pounded heavily beneath her soapy palms and
Miranda smiled, working lower, caressing him, soothing that hard, taut body as she moved. She traced the
healing scars on his thigh, mourning his pain, and the
vision of Gabriel taking the cougar's charge shot icily
through her for just a moment. Then rising, she came
against him, sleek and soft. She held that hungry
black gaze as she slid her arms around him to soap
his back.

"You're enjoying this. That I would come to you

first,'' he whispered roughly as the shower hissed
around them. He had not touched her, his hands
curled into fists at his side. His unsteady mood swept
through the steam, his wariness of her an excitement
that drew her on.

"You've never bathed with a woman, have you,
Gabriel?''

"No.'' The answer was curt and warning, yet telling her that he'd given her more intimacy than he
wished.

She strolled a fingertip down his cheek and circled
that grim mouth. "Turnabout is fair play, you know.''

Gabriel reached behind her and turned off the water. "But then, you've already had your shower,
haven't you?'' he asked, before shoving aside the
door and circling her with his arms, lifting her out.

She almost smiled at the hurried way he swished
the towel around her, as if she were his prize to carry
off, to claim. Just once he searched her expression.
"This is your mother's house,'' he noted unevenly.
"I would not want to dishonor Anna.''

"She would want you here—with me.''

He lightly tugged a damp strand of her hair. His
words were an uneven mix of whimsy and need, as
though he had dreamed of her. "I had hoped you
would be waiting in my bed.''

"I'm not a woman to wait, Gabriel. Especially not
now,'' she whispered and locked her arms around his
shoulders. He was warm and safe and strong against
her. She'd been terrified for him, afraid that this time
the cougar's fangs would find that muscled throat,
tearing—

"You need me.'' The tone was arrogant, masculine

and pleased, and Gabriel's grin teased her. Then that dark, fierce hunger coursed through his expression, his arms tugging her close. In the next heartbeat, Gabriel dived in to take—just as she wanted.

Whatever instinct that caused Gabriel to come straight to her, to need her to soothe him, Miranda rejoiced in the truth of that wonder. She reveled in how his hands roamed over her, shaking and possessing as they caressed. She met the fierce hunger of his mouth, fused to hers, slanting for a tighter fit, tongues playing, suckling. Suddenly he lifted her higher, her toes inches off the floor as he carried her, kissing her all the while, back to her bed.

Fire and flash, skin burning, Gabriel came down upon her. There was that hard hunter's look as he studied her, his hands possessing her, tormenting her. She did not fear that look, but reveled in it. Shaking with passion, she lifted to kiss his throat, to taste that dark, mysterious exotic skin. He inhaled roughly as she bit him gently, kissing the small wound. When she caught that flat nipple in her lips, tugging at it, Gabriel let out a muffled shout, jerking fractionally away from her.

In the shadows, his narrowed eyes burned at her as she arched beneath him. Gabriel's trembling hand slid down her hip, then to her thigh, stroking her. "You're a furnace, sweet Miranda."

She smoothed his long, powerful back, his firm buttocks and slid him a look. She loved being desired, flirting a bit, a game she'd never played. "Miss me, did you?"

Gabriel nuzzled her neck, her ears, her forehead and nibbled at her ears. He rubbed his chest side to side, looking as if he were luxuriating in the softness of her breasts, the hardened nipples etching his skin. There was that quick, hot look down at their bodies as if the sight gave him unexpected delight. ''I feared for my backside every step.''

She laughed at that, a wild, free joy soaring through her. Above her, Gabriel was too still, watching her and when the laughter faded, she met his hunger, his body coming sleekly into her keeping. The pounding hunger rose quickly, once, twice and Gabriel held her poised, tormenting her as the riveting pleasure tore her apart. ''Beast,'' she whispered shakily, her heart pounding violently.

He moved slowly then, surely, fulfilling them both and leaving her limp and breathless within his arms. His mouth leisurely roamed her breasts, then he turned her to her stomach, kissing a trail down to the small of her back. She tensed as those white teeth nipped her bottom lightly, playfully. Then he moved to cover her, his face pressed into her throat, his lips tantalizing. ''I think it is you who missed me.''

''Smug, arrogant—''

Then Gabriel turned her again and this time the taking was sweeter, almost dreamlike, until he rested gently upon her. She listened to the night and to her heart, and smiled, for this time, Gabriel could not deny whatever burned between them. He hadn't argued about what was best for her, or made any choices other than following his instincts. She kissed his forehead and smoothed that wonderful back, and wondered how his child would look, lying as closely to her breast.

In the morning, Miranda stood fully dressed in her

business slacks suit, studying the man in her bed. Clearly exhausted from his hunt and from the love-making throughout the night, Gabriel slept heavily. The flower print of her sheets and pillowcases only emphasized the dark power of his body, those rippling muscles as he sprawled. She couldn't resist bending to kiss the small of his back, admiring the cords and muscles that quivered from the light touch.

He'd come to her, not taking time to control his need to see her. That gift alone was enough to cause her to smile all the way to Noah Douglas's Investment Service office.

Later that morning, Gabriel stiffened as Koby Austin walked along beside him on Freedom's unique historical street, lined with two-story buildings. Koby sniffed the air. "Smells like spring flowers or a woman's shampoo—uh, oh, that's you, isn't it, Old Shot in the Butt."

Gabriel's dark look caused Koby to grin. "A legend in your own time. Shot by the woman who is courting you. Helpless as a baby— Okay, I see you're not exactly happy this morning."

When Koby strolled down to the Wagon Wheel for his morning coffee break, Gabriel glanced at the men on the street. Every one of them grinned back at him. Apparently the whole town knew of Miranda's ill-fated shot. Koby was right, Gabriel wasn't in a good mood. When he'd awakened, he'd expected Miranda to…his expectations were wrong. Tanner had explained that Miranda had taken two part-time jobs and her pickup was now parked beside Noah Douglas's sleek black Mercedes. John Lachlan at the bank was her other employer. Gabriel frowned, uncomfortable with his dark, surly mood. Both men were known wife-hunters and Miranda would be a match to either one.

He entered the feed store, and filled a small sack with beans for the garden she had tilled. He studied the bag and knew that Miranda could have her own garden at Anna's. Which would she choose? Would she come back to him?

Gabriel rubbed his jaw, considering the bins of seeds. He had not taken time to plant a garden, but then he hadn't had a woman to please, either. In quick order, he filled other sacks with lettuce, corn and squash. He glanced at the sticks that would become berries and thought of how Miranda enjoyed serving homemade wine, remembering her mother's recipes for jams. He added those to his purchase and John, the clerk, looked over his glasses at Gabriel. "Doing a little spring shopping before going hunting, are you? I see you're wearing those moccasins and you've got that sharp, eagle-eyed look as when you were tracking that renegade bear. Heard you got that cougar, and those photographers passing through town said the pictures of you tangling with it were going to be in the magazines. Reckon even celebrities take time to make spring gardens. You've never been in here buying seed before. It's a first garden for you, is it? Say, you never answered me. Are you going on another hunt?"

Gabriel thought of the woman he needed to see this morning, and nodded, then exited the feed store. He could have cooked her breakfast, tried for less head-on, demanding, possessive lover technique, immediately bedding her. Even a stallion might nuzzle a mare before mating.... He wanted to be affectionate, dammit. He opened the door to the office and removed his Western hat, holding it in one hand and his other arm filled with the sack of his feed store purchases.

Miranda stood next to Noah as they studied the paperwork columns on an ultramodern desk. Gabriel froze; they looked so much in tune, Miranda suiting the upscale look of Noah, her gray slacks suit expensive and fluid as she straightened. Her watch was slim and practical as was the dainty beaded chain around her throat. Her gray pumps said she liked comfort as she worked, the cream silk blouse completing the picture of a businesswoman not often seen in Freedom Valley. Her bright look, that rosy flush, reminded him of the passion they'd shared as he braced himself to— To do what? It was her right to choose her life, not his.

Would her former lover come for her? Would she take him again?

"Gabriel," Noah murmured, his gray eyes taking in Gabriel's clothing, his tracking moccasins, and the way his fist gripped his hat.

"Noah." Gabriel wished he had changed; Noah's three-piece suit was classy and expensive. His hands weren't rough and calloused, and his financial resources were enough to buy Miranda anything she wanted. Gabriel's fingers tightened on the paper sack and it rustled slightly. Miranda seemed like a creature from another world—sleek, modern, efficient—moving toward him. He was stunned by her kiss as she stood on tiptoe, her hand curving behind his head to draw his lips down to hers.

Gabriel trembled, shocked that she would exhibit such affection so openly. Her lips burned his and—Had he imagined that playful nip of her teeth? His heart leaped, bursting with pleasure, and when she drew away, he resisted the urge to pack her over his shoulder and take her home where she belonged. He pushed back that old-fashioned instinct to claim her, for he would have to learn new ways if he was to keep her, to please her. "You'll wait for me, won't you, Gabriel? I'll be just a little bit longer here and then I'd like to buy you lunch, if you have time?"

Time? He'd already waited a lifetime. Yet the custom of the woman to provide for him rankled. "I have time," he said, and eased into a chair in the waiting area.

She is a warrior, he thought, watching Miranda punch keys on her laptop, showing the results to Noah. A printer began to purr, spitting out paper, and Miranda whipped the list from the machine, studying it. She quickly circled items, recalculated the statistics and showed the results to Noah. Gabriel sucked in his breath as Noah bent over her desk, nodding as she showed him the results of her study. "You've done it. You've pinpointed the best balanced retirement fund mix that I can offer my farming and ranching clients. Make this a full-time job, Miranda, and you can name your price."

Noah hugged her briefly, took one look at Gabriel and cleared his throat. "I'll just take these back to the office and study them."

After he had gone, Miranda tugged up her suit sleeve, glanced at her watch and smiled. "Time for lunch. Ready, Gabriel?"

She frowned at the blond man entering the glass doors, careful of the huge wrapped presents he carried, topped by a toy panda bear. Dressed in a stylish black leather jacket, his crisp waving hair was neatly trimmed, his black sweater and flowing black pants were obviously tailored and expensive. His loafers were "city" and highly polished. He moved toward her, smiling warmly, clearly at home in the office setting.

"Scott," Miranda murmured softly, and Gabriel tensed at her tone. This was her former lover, a man who propped his designer sunglasses above his head. Gabriel noted the sleek red sports car parked outside.

At last, the father of her child had come to make amends. Gabriel breathed quietly, aware of Miranda's flush as she glanced at him. Rough and wearing his hunting clothing, he must look shabby in comparison to the well-groomed man she had loved, arms brimming with presents. The sack Gabriel held rustled—his gift to her of garden seeds and blackberry starts.

As they stood together, Miranda and the man, Gabriel thought that they were a matched pair—stylish, businesslike, expensive.

Then she stared at the gifts, the reminder of her lost baby obviously sharp and painful, the man's voice was smooth and cultured as he talked to her. Though the words were indistinct, the plea was there, a man trying to recover a treasure he had tossed away. Gabriel noted the pale color of her cheeks, the way her fingers gripped the toy bear, her expression rigid. She shook her head, her mouth moving, but the office was silent.

Gabriel could feel her pain—leaping within her,

tearing at her. He hadn't realized he was standing, moving toward her to protect her.

"It's my baby. I want to see it. You can't deny me that," Scott was saying. "Look, Miranda. I made a terrible mistake. My mother and dad want to know their grandchild. We'll work this out—"

"Will we?" Miranda's voice was hard, cutting through the shadows. "You're a little late, Scott. I lost the baby."

"You deliberately—" Scott swung to look at Gabriel, taking in his rough appearance. "Who's this?"

Gabriel smiled tightly and placed his sack on the floor. He stood slowly, and Miranda's eyes widened at the cold, silent threat. "You're not in this, Gabriel. I'll handle—"

"Am I not?" Gabriel's words were spaced and extremely careful.

"You don't waste any time, do you, Miranda?" Scott asked harshly. "Was it really my baby? Or his?"

Five seconds later, Scott stormed out of the glass doors, taking the presents with him. His red sports car roared out of Freedom.

Noah leaned against the wall, his arms folded, and grinned at Gabriel. "Well, that was something you don't see every day—Miranda slugging a man."

Gabriel grinned back as Miranda paced back and forth, muttering to herself, gesturing wildly with her hands. "True."

"She's got a mean right cross," Noah said. "I'd remember that, if I were you, Gabriel."

"I...am...a logical person, a lady, and...I have never, ever hit anyone like that before," Miranda said, shaking her head as if to clear it. Her hand trembled as she stared at it. "To think that he would have the nerve—"

Noah chuckled. "I bet he won't again, whatever he did."

"Men!" Miranda continued to pace and mutter and then glared at Gabriel. "I was only defending you. He could have hurt you."

At that Noah roared with laughter, doubling over. Miranda turned like a gunfighter, eyeing him and Noah blinked, his laughter dying. "What did I do?"

She frowned at Gabriel and took his jacket in both her fists, trying to shake him. "Don't say one word. And do not tell Kylie or Tanner about this. Do not tell anyone. I can't believe I— Uh!"

"Sometimes you talk too much," Gabriel said as he patted the soft backside draped over his shoulder. He took the sack Noah placed into his free arm and strolled through the open door, carrying Miranda.

On the street, Gabriel placed her on her feet, let her straighten her clothing and search furiously for words. Then he took her hand and drew it to his lips, sucking her fingers one by one as she stared, stunned, at him. "Thank you for defending me," he said softly and tried to smother his grin.

"Arrogant, hardheaded, muscle-bound— You can't just pick me up and tote me down half a block, saying 'Nice day, isn't it?' to anyone you meet, and—" Miranda paused, licked her lips and the look she gave him all the way down and all the way up caused his blood to heat. In his mind, he saw her nestled beside him, her body pale against his. He saw her laughing up at him, the wind tossing her hair, her cheeks rosy.

Miranda shivered and said, "If you keep looking at me like that, we won't make it to lunch. I'll have to cancel my afternoon job at John's bank."

"You like working with numbers, don't you? It's a game for you, isn't it?"

"I do...yes. But there are other things I enjoy, too. Something I do not enjoy is having you look at me in an office and watching your thoughts cross your face. You think I'm leaving, don't you? That I'm off to some fictitious high-paying job, some penthouse, some world without you."

"It is not for me to say," he stated carefully, because she had captured his thoughts too perfectly. He wasn't certain he liked her ability to interpret his expressions, especially when he thought he had them hidden. "But I would come to you, my woman, my heart."

"You can say the loveliest things," she whispered, studying him with that sultry look that said she, too, remembered their passion.

At the Wagon Wheel Café, Gabriel nodded at Fidelity who was stealthily considering Luigi as he circled Willa. "I see you two are working at this relationship. Five points, Gabriel. I saw how you squired Miranda down the street and held her hand. I worried about the lack of affection—those little demonstrative hugs and looks that are unique to people in love."

"It is for Miranda that I allow myself to be courted," Gabriel said stiffly, ill at ease with the thought that she would be paying for his meal.

"Of course. You are endearing yourself to all the Women of the Council by the way you are allowing her to set the rules. We had thought that you might be difficult in accepting our traditions. You're very old-fashioned in your way, too."

"I may change the rules, but it does not mean that they are less honored," Gabriel warned softly, and was unprepared for Fidelity's delighted chuckle.

"But of course," she said as if she had expected him to challenge the Founding Mothers' traditions.

When they were seated in a booth, Gabriel placed the feed store sack on the seat beside him. He stiffened when Miranda's foot slid up his leg and her toes rested intimately on his thigh. He reached for her foot, caressing it. "Having fun?"

She grinned and his heart leaped again, filled with sunshine. "More than you know. What's in the sack?"

"Beans...corn...blackberry starts...for you." He was embarrassed that he had not brought a gift more suiting a lover.

"For me?" Miranda's delighted tone caused Gabriel to relax slightly. "How did you know? Oh, I..." She stood slightly, bent over the booth and reached for him. Her kiss left Gabriel shaking and dazed. He leaned back in the booth, tried to breathe and tried to stop from glowing as Miranda carefully unpacked the small sacks from the large one, lining them up on the booth's table.

"This morning, I emptied the rest of your mother's jars and washed them."

Her eyes were shimmering with tears. "You knew how difficult that was for us, how much we missed her."

"It was a small thing to do."

"No, it wasn't. It was very, very thoughtful.

Mother's jars were so special to her. She took great care with them. Some of them came from her mother. I missed canning with her, filling those jars. Every cucumber had to be standing upright, matched in size, for dill pickles, the bread and butter sweet pickles sliced exactly right. A handful of less than ripe strawberries added to the jam mix, to keep the taste more fresh. Green beans had to be snapped just so. Nothing was wasted, even the green tomatoes were pickled before the frost came. She had such a hard financial time after Dad died. But she raised us without a complaint.''

Gabriel took her hands and bent to place his face within them. The tenderness in the gesture was unreserved, for Gabriel was a caring man. She knew he grieved with her, understood her heart. She knew he feared for her passage, for the day when the world challenged her again and she would leave him.

Sally Jo, the waitress appeared to take their order, pad in hand. ''Oh, my goodness. He is just so romantic. I saw him carry you out of the office. I'd love to have a man come for me like that, leaving no doubt to me or anyone else that he wanted me.''

Gabriel straightened, still holding Miranda's hands in his. His smile at Sally Jo was devastating. ''I am certain that, as lovely as you are, you have many men wanting you.''

Sally Jo stared blankly at him, then she blurted, ''I heard you didn't like women. That you were a mountain man avoiding female companionship. But how you do sweet-talk.''

Miranda studied Gabriel's charming smile, and his dark, contemplative look at her. She didn't trust that secretive, pleased-with-himself look, or the too-innocent one that followed it.

That look lasted throughout lunch, and Gabriel didn't object when she paid the bill as she had expected. He walked her to the bank and her afternoon job, bent to kiss her cheek as though he were a friend, not a lover. She'd expected a kiss to match his tenderness earlier, and yet the brush of his lips was almost impersonal. He strolled off down the street without another look back at her.

Miranda watched him, her hands on her waist. Gabriel had his edges, his moods and his games. She wasn't certain she'd forgiven him yet, for all those years they'd lost. Or for not giving her that kiss.

That night, he came to her again, leaving no doubt of his wildfire passion for her. She met him out there on that naked, hot plane, where every touch seared, every pulse and heartbeat matched, riveting and devouring them. And in the morning, Gabriel was gone.

Ten

There comes a time when what was important
isn't any longer, replaced by truth. If love is at
the bottom of the barrel, then it must be freed
and cleaned and polished and met and brought
into the daylight.

Anna Bennett's Journal

Fully dressed for work, wearing a white short sleeve
sweater beneath her black pantsuit, Miranda studied
the sack of seedlings and packages of bulk garden
seeds. Gabriel's gift said she could choose where to
make her life and where to live it, as she wished—
planting where she wished, or not. Her tiny tomato
seedlings stretched toward morning sunlight, and her
mother's pantry was neatly lined with clean jars.

It was April now, the earth bursting with promise,

sunshine dancing on the newly budded leaves in her
mother's garden. Delicate small white Lily of the
Valley blooms would soon appear, leading the way
for the scarlet bleeding hearts. It was as if the earth
waited for her to move forward, to know herself, and
place the past behind her.

Miranda leaned back into the kitchen filled with
memories, tears filling her eyes, her throat tightening
with emotion. On the counter, the blackberry starts
were no longer dried looking sticks, but had begun to
sprout green leaves. Their roots needed to be set in
firm, nourishing soil, just as she needed to set the
foundation for her life.

Who courted whom? she asked herself, for Gabriel
had come to her every night, the taste of hunger on
his lips, the trembling of his hands telling her of his
need. During the day, as she punched in numbers,
calculated statistics and waited for the night, Miranda
caught herself dreaming of him—the way he touched
her, that dark closed look that said he had secrets of
his own. Miranda placed her hand on her heart, listened to the beat, and knew that her time had come—
Until now, she wasn't ready to read her mother's jour-
nals, too filled with mourning to bear the encounter.

But now it was time, and she picked up the telephone to call Noah and take the day off. Curling up
on her mother's couch, Miranda opened the worn
books, her mother's handwriting curving through
them.

"Truth, above all, must be met, good or bad. When
a woman chooses her path, a good man will wait for
her decision. That is hard for the male species—waiting, when their very nature says to stake their claim.

But when a woman finds her truth, knows it in her heart, she should hold it dear and meet it full force. She will battle all odds to keep it safe," Anna had written. "I worry about Miranda, for she is trying too hard to please everyone, but herself. She has a bright, quick mind, and needs challenges. A woman's battles are not always in business and money, but sometimes she has to listen to her heart."

Miranda held the journal close to her heart. She had watched her mother widowed, trying to provide for her family. Miranda studied so hard to achieve, to win those scholarships, to help her mother. She was a girl, fearing failure, pushing too hard. She'd dived into everything the community expected her to be— an honors student, witty, vivacious, filling her life with everything youth had to offer. At seventeen, she wouldn't have been ready for marriage, and her mother knew. Gabriel knew.

Two hours later, the midmorning sun slanted through the pine trees lining the road to Gabriel's ranch. She reached out her free hand and gripped the sack with the blackberry bushes and the seeds. Only Gabriel would understand how she needed to fill herself, just as she would fill her mother's canning jars. The need to see him, to tell him what she now understood, was urgent, but the eagerness of coming home leaped through her, too. It had been two weeks since she'd seen it, the log cabin nestled in the woods, the huge old weathered barn in the field. She'd been too intent upon getting back into the flow of work, mentally drained when she returned home. The weekends were filled with Gabriel, staying at her house, with family and friends, as she slid back into life in Freedom Valley.

The garden she had plowed had been tilled; the neat fence around it would keep it safe. In the field, calves played, and twenty of Gabriel's Appaloosa fed on the huge bales of hay—the new grass not enough yet to support them.

She had to tell him.

Miranda glanced at the framework of a new addition onto Gabriel's simple, but large log home. She parked her pickup and hurried inside, finding the house empty, his camera bag gone. Jessica didn't move from her couch pillow, eyeing Miranda. "I don't have time for catering to you now," Miranda said and stepped outside. In the distance, higher on the mountain, Fletcher's bark was faint but distinctive. She smiled briefly, recognizing the dog's sound as he played with his master.

She had to tell Gabriel.

The sun, high in the sky, signaled noon. She stripped away her light denim jacket, tying it around her waist and scanned the woods, pine and fir and brush shielding Gabriel from her. She opened the top buttons of her cotton blouse, and picked the briars from her torn jeans. On a high ledge, overlooking his ranch, Miranda placed her hand over her eyes, scanning the thick woods. Fletcher was quiet now, giving her no clues.

Birds darted over the high mountain meadow, with its yellow-green new grass. Coming up from the valley, warmer in winter than the mountains, a herd of deer bolted into the woods. Gabriel's tripod and camera were set up near a blanket and she scanned the dark, mysterious woods for him. "Gabriel?"

Then a tall shadow slid silently into the clearing and Gabriel said, "Why are you here?"

She should have known he'd watched her; these mountains were his home. She wanted the words to come, willed them to her lips and failed. "I have to talk with you."

"Talk." The order gave no softening encouragement, as if Gabriel braced himself for a hard blow. He crossed his arms over his bare chest, the muscles taut beneath his gleaming dark skin. One hard look took in her blouse, her jeans and the moccasins he had made, a feminine match for the ones he wore.

She knew he expected her to leave, to find a high-paying job such as the ones she'd had, filled with marvelous challenges to be met. Why were the words so difficult?

"You've waited for me, all this time." Her statement was breathless with wonder.

He nodded slowly, his stance wary, his hair gleaming and tossed by the light April breeze as it crossed the highland meadow. "You were my vision, the woman in the smoke. I could do no less."

She scratched Fletcher's ears when he leaned heavily against her, pressing his need for affection. Miranda met Gabriel's dark, intense stare, his expression taut, those beautiful lips tightened. "You were right all those years ago, Gabriel. I needed to prove myself against the world. I needed to make the journey, and I needed to come home to you."

He inhaled sharply, muscles tightening across his broad chest, the bright sunlight skimming those powerful shoulders. Only the pulse running down his dark throat gave away his deep emotion.

"I would never have known who I was, the person that I am now, if I hadn't gone to college, succeeded at my career. Had you not made that decision, all those years ago, we might have married. All that talk from the school counselor and principal, the tests I'd taken to confirm my potential, might have haunted me later. It could have torn us apart. I might have resented what I'd never done or seen. Now I know, without doubt, that my path is with yours. Here, in these mountains with you."

He nodded slowly, watching her with that wary expression, those marvelous eyes shielded by his glossy long lashes. She walked those few feet to him. "You are a spiritual man, Gabriel. Your essence is here in these mountains. You gave me time, when you had none, letting me find my own path, leading back to you. Yet nothing has really changed between us since you gave me that wildflower bouquet. You tore away my heart, only to give it back to me stronger than before, more certain of my life."

He swallowed roughly, and she knew that he was waiting for her to finish. She placed her palm over his heart, and it leaped, racing into her keeping. "You are my challenge, Gabriel, my excitement that will never end."

"You will become my wife?" he asked unevenly, the shiver racking his tall body telling her of his uncertainty.

"Yes." She smiled up at him, bursting with joy and loving him. "Your grandmother, White Fawn, told you that long ago, didn't she?"

He nodded gravely. "She knew my vision would be true, and that my heart could belong to no other. But she knew that you were headstrong and independent and the pressures were on you to go to college and to succeed. She said a long journey awaited you and I could not influence your passage. I could only wait for you to make it. Then when you were so ill, I could wait no longer to claim you, to care for you. I wished it were true, that the child was mine and that he had lived."

She touched his cheek, skimming the rugged contours, those high, gleaming cheekbones, that strong jaw, his incredible tender mouth. "Tell me of the first time you made love to me."

Was it only a short time ago? Yet she remembered his trembling touch, the way his body hesitated, then those first still moments within her keeping as if he were uncertain. "Just now, you said White Fawn told you your vision was true. You are not an undiscriminating man, bedding any woman for your body's needs, and you have said that you tried. Then, I thought you feared for me, for my healing body. Now, I think it was that and something else."

Gabriel's expression closed, and she knew she had hit her mark. "That's quite some case," he noted darkly. "Cannot a man keep one secret, or must you have it, too?"

"Tell me, so that I have everything," she whispered, loving him even more.

His hands rose to stroke her hair, lifting the strands to gleam in the sunlight, blue-black as a raven's wing. Then he bent to her, his lips brushing hers. "I was already married, in my heart. How could I share my body with another woman, when it belonged to you?''

He kissed the tears shimmering on her lashes, brought by joy and love. ''You are my first and only love. That time was my first, and yet, I knew it could never be like that with another woman. I feared so that I would hurt you, that my body would bolt from my keeping. I will never forget that moment we became one.''

With the truth sweet upon the fresh mountain air, the sunshine dancing around them and in her heart, Miranda eased open the jacket's sleeves, knotted at her waist. ''Love me now,'' she whispered, suddenly shy of him, for he was new to her, this Gabriel, the man of her heart.

His fingertip skimmed the heat of her cheeks, then slid to her throat, and lower to open the buttons of her blouse. He undressed her solemnly, reverently, until she stood proudly before him, the woman that she had become.

Her hands moved over him, their gazes locked as his clothing fell to the meadow's new spring grass. His touch trembled, skimming her body, treasuring it as he bent to take her lips carefully, gently with his own. ''So long I have waited for you,'' he whispered unevenly as she slid her arms around him.

He swept her up in his arms, carrying her to the blanket he had used earlier, lowering her to it. He was her promise, her dream, her heart, coming to her. There would be other times, when hunger drove them to the crest, eager for the heat and fire. But now with the sunlight warming them, the scent of spring touching them, Gabriel entered her wordlessly, his body telling her of his love, of the truth running between them. Over her, his expression was tender. "The river of my love for you will never stop flowing."

She would carry those words with her forever, she thought before giving herself to the sweet taking.

Gabriel waited for Miranda to come to him. He leaned against his pickup, filled with items from Anna's house. Michael's and Tanner's pickups were also filled. The day had been long for Miranda, working with her brother and sister to separate her mother's things. It was a task each had placed aside, but the time had come to work together, each considerate of the other. Gabriel scanned Anna's two-story home, wrapped in the first of May sunlight; some of the contents had been divided among Tanner, Kylie and Miranda. It had been a hard day for each of them, memories swirling through the house, Anna's presence held close and dear. Anna's jars and canning necessities, her favorite pots and pans had been divided between the Bennett sisters and the jars would soon be in the addition's new pantry. Women's things, Gabriel thought, passed from mother to daughter, would be cherished in the Bennetts' new homes.

With the help of their friends and family, the new addition onto his home was more suiting a wife and a family. Miranda had worked beside him, though he disdained her helping, and each night she came softly to his bed.

She'd turned furiously on him once, when he tried to take a board from her. "My mother worked beside my father. You would expect less from me? Who do you think you are?"

He could think of no answer, except to tug her
close and slant his lips over hers, igniting them both.
"That's who you are," he'd managed shakily later,
and for the sake of modesty took the board and placed
it strategically in front of his hips.

"Okay," she'd said just as unevenly, her face
flushed. "I'm taking a shower and I'm going to bed."

His mouth had dried, his body leaping into the fever that she had called forth. "Miranda. It is noon."

The air had sizzled between them, and Gabriel had
forgotten about everything but carrying her off to his
bed.

As he stood in Anna's driveway now, Gabriel
tucked that memory away to savor later. Gently
rounded with Michael's child, Kylie hugged Miranda.
Holding Anna's patchwork quilt tightly, Gwyneth's
small body was ripe with the baby that would arrive
in another month. Tanner paused, carrying a box of
Anna's clothing to be donated to charity. He glanced
at Gabriel and at Michael, also caught by the scene.

Anna's three children had been through hardships,
and had survived, returning to Freedom Valley, where
she had found so much peace and love. Now that
peace and love would go on in their homes, small
memories of her tucked into each piece of furniture,
each doily, each quilt.

Because Tanner had learned carpentry from his father, and as a boy had worked with his father's tools,
they were now his. Gwyneth moved toward Tanner,
leaning her head against his shoulder, the gesture said
she understood his sadness. They looked so complete.

Michael's arm was now around Kylie, his head
bent to hers. She leaned heavily against him, and he

swept her up in his arms placing her inside his pickup. Kylie snuggled close to Michael, his arm still around her as they pulled out onto the main road.

Gwyneth's hand smoothed Tanner's back as he carried the tools into the new building where he built custom boats.

Then Miranda walked toward Gabriel, her head bent. He lifted her face and kissed the tears away. "She's always going to be with you and Kylie and Tanner."

"I think—when it is time, there will be a need for her house." Miranda's forehead bent and she came to rest against him in the old way, that told him her grief ran deep. "Take me home, Gabriel."

At the ranch, Miranda didn't go into the house. Instead she walked to the garden they had planted together, a row of bright green lettuce just beginning to sprout. Miranda was placing the past behind her, keeping the good and discarding the ugly, preparing to move on in her life. Gabriel came behind her, folding her tight against him in the setting sunlight.

"I want our wedding here," Miranda said quietly, turning to him. "And soon. What do you think?"

How could he refuse her anything, this woman of his heart? He nodded, meeting her searching gaze. "Are you finished courting me?"

"I've just begun," she whispered, and stood on tiptoe to brush her lips against his. "I've just begun," she repeated softly. "Your dad is loaning me his best wagon and four-horse team."

Gabriel frowned, holding her away to study her impish grin. "You're not handling his four-horse team."

"Your mother does."

He shook his head, rummaging for reasons why Miranda should not manage the powerful horses. He decided to retreat; images of Miranda driving a wagon with him sitting beside her nettled. She had paid for the tickets to the Firemen's Spring Ball and for the dinners at the Wagon Wheel, and for the drinks at the Silver Dollar. "I'd better start unpacking the pickup."

"It can wait. You're upset and have that closed-in look."

"I'm going to the barn," he said, and realized that he was being unfair. Miranda was only following the customs of Freedom Valley.

Moments later, Miranda stepped into the barn, finding him immediately. "Let's have this out. You're a beautiful, caring man, but you're growling about the Rules of Bride Courting."

"I have the book Fidelity demanded I read." This discussion was unpleasant, and Gabriel did not like thinking about how many men had chafed under the town's unique custom, which had protected pioneer women.

"I haven't asked you to marry me yet, Gabriel Deerhorn. *You* have asked me, but *I* have not asked *you*," she underlined.

That ungentle reminder that in Freedom Valley, women had always determined their fate and protected other women, caused Gabriel to frown. He walked slowly to her and Miranda's green eyes widened as he leaned down to whisper. "Ask me."

"Not under these circumstances. I have a candle-light dinner planned."

Gabriel tugged on a strand of her hair and placed his lips near hers, whispering, ''Ask me.''

She shivered and flattened against the wall and he placed both hands beside her head, corralling her. ''Ask me.''

He nudged his knee between her jeaned legs, and whispered against her throat, ''Ask me.''

He kissed her slowly, thoroughly, his hand unbuttoning her blouse. Her bra tore easily, freeing her breasts to his roaming touch. She shivered as his thumbs cruised over her hardened nipples, his kiss deepening, his knee lifted to nudge her intimate warmth. It was a new game he had grown to love, seducing her, testing her, waiting for her to ignite.

Miranda's fingers locked onto his shirt, her color rising, those dark green eyes sultry upon him. ''You love doing this to me, don't you?''

''And you love doing it to me?''

''Maybe,'' she whispered lightly.

Still she resisted, driving him on, passion dancing between them. Gabriel bent to take her breast, suckling as his other hand unsnapped her jeans and slid into her briefs.

She came quickly into his passion, warm and throbbing and arching against him, her mouth hot with the fever driving them both. In his plan to seduce her, Gabriel had not planned to be taken so quickly, the fire igniting as he filled his hands with her bare hips. Her hands fumbled with his clothing and then released, he filled her slowly, fully.

She held him tightly, answering his primitive call, matching him for strength, taking his mouth, feeding upon him as he tasted her. He was flying now, Miranda breathing unevenly, her heart pounding him, her body greedy for his. He filled his fist with her hair, tugging her head back gently, watching her passion flow through her, and she took it inside, nourishing his own with that fierce, wild desperation.

She fought to contain her release, and he could not have that, pushing her, holding his own pounding passion.

Later, he would hold her still, uncertain of what she would do. He had taken her primitively, fed by his own hunger. Miranda's heart still raced against his own, her body limp and soft, draped around him. Humor filled her tone as she said, "Okay. If that's how you really feel about it, I'll ask you. In your way, you can be a real rat, but I love you anyway. You're getting very good at seduction, slow or fast."

He smiled at that, loving the exciting game that would continue all their lives. "What's that? I can't hear you," he teased.

He looked down at their bodies, hers pale and soft against his, a beautiful, wonderful sight. His body was already hardening, filling her again. "It seems I need to make up for lost time," he whispered in an apology.

She watched him carefully, a tender smile curving her kiss-swollen lips. "Will you marry me, Gabriel?"

Gabriel waited for his wife to come to him as the mid-May night sounds cruised their mountain campsite. At their wedding, Fidelity Moore had kissed him soundly, shocking him. "This is a fine example of a husband. You unmarried boys take note of how he accepted his love's courtship."

Miranda, dressed in the doeskin beaded shift that his grandmother had made for her long ago, had shot him a disbelieving look. For Gabriel had loved every moment, playing the game of seduction with his love, watching her blush and run and tease and love him wildly.

He sighed, taking his happiness into him to cherish. Soon his wife's body would change, her breasts becoming fuller, her body softening and rounding with their child. He would treasure each moment, each change, for White Fawn had said that their first baby would be created on their wedding night. He rubbed the fullness in his heart, and wondered how such joy could come to him, how Miranda could love so freely and openly, sometimes shocking him.

His smile grew as he studied the starlit Montana night. Some things were better not shared, he decided. Miranda would want to tell him in her own way of their child. White Fawn had held up four fingers, indicating the children that would carry on his blood and his father's father's long after he was gone. But each time, he would wait for Miranda to tell him, to bring him her excitement and joy.

Well, then, he thought, turning toward their campfire, studying their future in it, he would build a home office for her, enlarging their home once more. If her numbers called to her, she would have what she needed. If she needed to work away from their home, he would tend their brood. For he had waited for so long....

Then standing beyond the fire and the smoke, Miranda appeared. She found him in the night, and slowly removed the doeskin wedding shift. It pooled at her feet, leaving the firelight and the moonbeams flowing upon her face, her shoulders, her breasts. Shadows dancing within the firelight traced her hips and long legs, but he knew the strength of them, the beauty of those curves. He'd seen her without clothing, but his body stirred quickly, waiting to take her as his wife.

The smoke curled between them, drifting high into the night sky as Gabriel watched the Miranda of his visions, his wife, come to him.

He had waited so long....

* * * * *

*Don't miss Cait London's
next powerful love story,*

A LOVING MAN,

*where a rich, handsome
widower wins the trust of a wary,
small town woman.*

*On sale August 2001
from Silhouette Desire.*

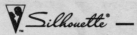

Meet 50 loving dads in

babies
& BACHELORS USA

Take 4 FREE BOOKS, Plus get a FREE GIFT!

Babies & Bachelors USA is a heartwarming new collection of reissued novels featuring 50 sexy heroes from every state who experience the ups and downs of fatherhood and find time for love all the same. All of the books, hand-picked by our editors, are outstanding romances by some of the world's bestselling authors, including Stella Bagwell, Kristine Rolofson, Judith Arnold and Marie Ferrarella!

Don't delay, order today! Call customer service at 1-800-873-8635.

Or

Clip this page and mail it to The Reader Service:

In U.S.A.
P.O. Box 9049
Buffalo, NY
14269-9049

In CANADA
P.O. Box 616
Fort Erie, Ontario
L2A 5X3

YES! Please send me four FREE BOOKS and FREE GIFT along with the next four novels on a 14-day free home preview. If I like the books and decide to keep them, I pay just $15.96* U.S. or $18.00* CAN., and there's no charge for shipping and handling. Otherwise, I'll keep the 4 FREE BOOKS and FREE GIFT and return the rest. If I decide to continue, I'll receive six books each month—two of which are always free—until I've received the entire collection. In other words, if I collect all 50 volumes, I will have paid for 32 and received 18 absolutely free!

267 HCK 453
467 HCK 453

Name	(Please Print)		
Address			Apt. #
City	State/Prov.		Zip/Postal Code

* Terms and prices subject to change without notice.
 Sales Tax applicable in N.Y. Canadian residents will be charged applicable provincial taxes and GST. All orders are subject to approval.

DIRBAB01R   © 2000 Harlequin Enterprises Limited

invites you to enter the
exclusive, masculine world of the…

**Silhouette Desire's powerful miniseries features five
wealthy Texas bachelors—all members of the state's
most prestigious club—who set out to recover the
town's jewels…and discover their true loves!**

MILLIONAIRE M.D.—January 2001
by Jennifer Greene (SD #1340)

WORLD'S MOST ELIGIBLE TEXAN—February 2001
by Sara Orwig (SD #1346)

LONE STAR KNIGHT—March 2001
by Cindy Gerard (SD #1353)

HER ARDENT SHEIKH—April 2001
by Kristi Gold (SD #1358)

TYCOON WARRIOR—May 2001
by Sheri WhiteFeather (SD #1364)

Available at your favorite retail outlet.

Where love comes alive™